Christy

Christy

Catherine Marshall

Adapted by
Anna Wilson Fishel

Fleming H. Revell
A Division of Baker Book House Co
Grand Rapids, Michigan 49516

Published by Fleming H. Revell
a division of Baker Book House Company
P.O. Box 6287, Grand Rapids, MI 49516-6287

Printed in the United States of America

Library of Congress Cataloging-in-Publication Data

Marshall, Catherine.
  Christy : adapted by Anna Wilson Fishel.
    p. cm.
  Summary: An adaptation of the 1967 novel chronicling the experiences
of a young woman after she arrives in a small mountain town in Ten-
nessee in 1912 to teach school.
  ISBN 0-8007-1708-2
  [1. Teachers—Fiction. 2. Schools—Fiction. 3. Christian life—Fiction.
4. Mountain life—Fiction.] I. Marshall, Catherine, 1914-1983.
Christy. II. Title.
  PZ7.F49885Ch   1995
  [Fic]—dc20   94-43919

The original movie *Christy* is now available on home video.

The Characters

Christy Rudd Huddleston, a nineteen-year-old girl
Alice Henderson, a Quaker mission worker from
  Ardmore, Pennsylvania
David Grantland, the young minister
Ida Grantland, the spinster sister of David
Dr. Neil MacNeill, the physician of the Cove
Jeb Spencer, a ballad-singing mountain man
Fairlight Spencer, Jeb's wife
  Their children: John, Zady, Clara, Lulu, and Little
  Guy
Bob Allen, the keeper of the mill by Blackberry
  Creek
Mary Allen, Bob's superstitious wife
  Their children: Rob, Festus, Creed, Della May,
  Nuda, Little Burl
Ault Allen, Bob's older brother, head of the clan
John Holcombe, a mountain man
Elizabeth Holcombe, John's wife
  Their children: Arrowood, Lizette, John, Sam
  Houston, baby girl
Uncle Bogg McHone, the county squire, humorist
  of Cutter Gap, teller of tall tales

Tom McHone, one of Uncle Bogg's grown sons
Opal McHone, Tom's wife
   Their children: Isaak, Toot, Vincent
Mountie O'Teale, a schoolchild
Ozias Holt, a mountain man
Rebecca Holt, Ozias's wife
   Their children: Wraight, Zacharias, Becky, Will,
   Dicle, Larmie, Jake, Vella
Bird's Eye Taylor, a feuder and blockader
Lundy Taylor, Bird's Eye's seventeen-year-old son
Ruby Mae Morrison, a girl who lives at the mission
   house
Ben Pentland, the mailman

1

Smoke poured out of the black smokestack. The conductor pulled the loud whistle, and Old Buncombe sputtered and wheezed with a choo . . . choo . . . choo. My train car jerked forward, and the one behind slammed into it. Finally the jerking and bumping smoothed out.

I was on my own at last. Feelings of excitement and adventure pulsed through my veins. As the telephone poles sped past my window, I looked around the railroad car. There was that certain smell of coal dust. I spotted three brass spittoons along the aisle and a potbellied stove in the rear. Sacks of grain and produce had been piled toward the back. I marveled that so many people had gotten up to catch a train at six-thirty on a Sunday morning.

A conductor in a faded blue suit approached my seat. "Ticket, please. You're Christy Huddleston, aren't you?"

The old man put his hand out for my ticket. "Bound for El Pano?"

"I'm going to teach school in Cutter Gap, seven miles from El Pano." I leaned down to scoot my suitcase closer on the floor beside me, out of his way.

The gentleman rubbed his chin whiskers and thought for a moment. "That Cutter Gap is right rough country, I hear. Last week, a man shot another man in the back because he got tired of shootin' turkeys at a turkey shoot. You'd best be careful." The conductor went on gathering tickets.

I was glad to be left alone with my thoughts. I glanced at the window to see my reflection. A slender, young lady with blue eyes and piled-up brown hair stared back at me. I was going to miss my home and my family. I really loved Asheville with its teas and parties and shops. I could almost smell my mother's bread baking in our big warm oven. I could see my brother, George, stumbling down the stairs to the landing each morning to lean on the banister and talk. And my father, he was turning grey now. I knew he loved me even though he didn't really think a nineteen-year-old girl should go off alone, especially on a wild adventure like teaching in a mountain cove.

I had tried to explain to them that I had to go. After meeting Dr. Ferrand last summer during our vacation near Asheville, I knew what I had to do. The elderly man with his clipped white goatee had stood in front of the auditorium and spoken about his medical mission in the Great Smoky Mountains. His words had inspired me. He told us the mountain people were poor but intelligent. The doctor was looking for volunteers to help these people. It was almost as if something had made me go up and talk with the doctor that day.

And now it was five months later, January 1912. With each turn of Old Buncombe's wheels, I was being carried closer and closer to a new life. It was late in the day when we crossed from North Carolina into Tennessee. The sun was sinking as the railroad tracks ran between the walls of a narrow valley. The train began to slow down, and the engineer blew a long warning whistle.

"El Pano!" the conductor announced as he lit the lanterns on the floor at the front of the coach. Old Buncombe's wheels ground to a stop.

The conductor was at the step as I got off the train. "Let me help you," he said, taking my suitcase and swinging it to the ground beside the train. "You watch yourself there in Cutter Gap, Miss Huddleston."

"All aboard!" The train once again began getting up a head of steam. As I stood on the platform with my hands in my muff, I watched the little white puffs from the engine get smaller against the grey sky. Fear gripped my heart. Everything dear and familiar to me was disappearing over that horizon with the train.

What would I do now? Shouldn't someone be meeting me? I waited but no one came. At last, I swallowed the lump in my throat, gripped my suitcase, and headed through the snow for the boarding house across the street.

No one came to get me from Cutter Gap, so I spent the night at the boarding house. The landlady told me about Mr. Pentland, the mailman, who was often at the

General Store. Early the next morning, I walked to the store to find him.

The smell of strong cheese and tobacco filled the air as I walked in. A group of men were whittling and rocking around a warm fire in the wood stove. I crossed the creaky floor and noticed a tall man in overalls and a grey shirt with a torn jacket. He was lacing his high boots.

"Excuse me," I said to the woman arranging spools of thread in a glass cabinet, "I was told I might find Mr. Pentland here."

The woman glanced at the tall man. "Ben Pentland," she called loudly, "come here, will ya?"

The leathery man looked over at me. His face was thin, and his bushy eyebrows nearly covered his eyes. He finished tying his boots, stood up, and walked over.

"Howdy," he said as he took my mittened hand. "I'm Ben Pentland."

"Mr. Pentland," I came right to the point, "could you help me? I arrived yesterday to teach school in Cutter Gap and thought someone would meet me, but no one has. Mrs. Tatum at the boarding house said you might help me get there since you carry the mail."

The man's thin lips and deep eyes got hard. "Don't know 'bout takin' no woman," he replied. "Wouldn't be fittin'." The postman paused for a moment and scratched his narrow nose. "Letters been pilin' up though. Got six to deliver today."

I caught myself before saying anything. *What kind of place is this,* I wondered, *where six letters are "piled-up" mail?*

"Please?" I almost begged. "I'll keep up with you. I only have one suitcase, and I can walk really fast."

"Well—" he scratched his rough face. "Kin you be ready in ten minutes?"

"I'm ready now," I replied.

Half an hour later Mr. Pentland and I were nearly at the first mailbox.

"Got one letter for the Becks. Their mailbox is just the other side of the Big Mud Hole," the mailman announced.

I picked up my long wool skirt and hurried to keep up with him. "Aren't all the mud holes frozen over by now?" I panted as my breath formed clouds in the stinging January cold.

"Shorely," the mailman replied. "Only this ain't just any old mud hole. This is the *Big* Mud Hole. In the spring, it's a sight to behold. Wagons sink right up to their axles, and mules might just as well be tryin' to hoof it through molasses."

I slowed down a little to shake the hem of my coat free from the wet, clinging snow. The white fields surrounding us reminded me of the white frosting on my mother's devil's food cakes. Then I saw the huge mud hole.

"Why don't the road men fix this hole?" I asked, as we made our way around it.

"Ain't no road men, Miz Huddleston," Mr. Pentland replied as he shifted my suitcase to his other hand. "We have to fix the roads ourselves out here." The mailman stopped before a mailbox sitting on a high stump.

"Here's the Beck's place," he said. "U-ni-ted States ma-il!" he almost yodelled.

11

As we walked down the road I looked back to spy an old woman wearing a tattered dress with a woolen shawl around her shoulders. She tromped through the snow to get the precious letter.

Soon the wide trail began to narrow and wind upwards. By now I realized that it took this mountain man only a few steps to cover what would be the length of a city block back in Asheville. I'd never walked seven miles at one time before, but I was keeping up with him. The Tennessee mountaineer seemed to know exactly where he was going, and I was glad. If it hadn't been for him, I'd never have found my way to Cutter Gap.

"Mr. Pentland, how many families live around Cutter Gap?" I was full of questions about this place I'd never seen.

The mailman thought for a moment. "Maybe 'bout seventy."

"Most of the people are farmers, aren't they?"

"Raise young'uns mostly," he answered slowly.

"Do most of the children go to the mission school where I'll be teaching?"

"Hit depends. Some goes and some don't. Not all of 'em got religion. But most of 'em seem to like the new preacher, David Grantland."

"Has he been at the mission long?" I asked as I struggled through a ditch.

"Near about three months. He's from somewhere up north."

"What's Miss Henderson like?" Alice Henderson was the missionary working with Dr. Ferrand. She was starting the school at Cutter Gap.

"Well, Miz Alice is a Quaker woman, you know, from Pennsylvania. Rides a horse all over the mountains by herself, sidesaddle, with a long skirt. Keeps busier than a honeybee round a rose bush—teachin', visitin' folks, and nursin' the sick. She's a smiley woman. All her wrinkles is smile wrinkles. And she wears her hair in braids folded round and round her head like—like a crown. She's sorta different."

"How's she different?" I prodded.

"Likes to talk about God," the mailman answered. "'God wants us all to be happy,' she's always a-sayin'. I could most believe it, watchin' her. She practices what she preaches."

By now, we had been walking an hour and a half. The trail was so narrow we had to walk single file. I carefully stepped into each one of Mr. Pentland's big boot tracks. Another hour of steady walking brought us to a second mountain. I panted as I tried to keep up. This path had been sliced out of the side of the mountain. To our left, the ledge dropped off into space. It must have been five hundred feet to the valley floor below. I could hear a cow-bell tinkling somewhere down there.

My eyes were watering, and my cheeks were stinging from the cold. I couldn't feel my toes inside my rubber boots, and I was getting tired. My skirts, wet almost to my knees, were now half-frozen. Even my eyelashes were beaded with wet snow.

"This here's Lonesome Pine Ridge." The cold wind carried the mailman's words back to my ears. "The wind's bad, but we're just about to the Spencers. They're on the other side of the ridge, near the top."

13

My heart was beating my chest like a drum. I felt sick to my stomach. I had never liked heights. With a gulp, I glanced at the top of the ridge. My heart sank. The tiny cabin perched up there seemed miles away. Would we ever get there? Just then, a strong gust of wind swept up from the north shoving me toward the ledge. I stumbled.

2

Mr. Pentland caught me by the arm just in time and helped me up. He let me hang on the rest of the way.

The Spencer cabin was made of rough logs chinked with mud. An old black pot, a crude wooden sled, and a tall pile of logs for firewood cluttered the yard. A dozen squawking chickens pecked in the snow. As we approached the split rail fence, yapping hounds raced toward us. A scruffy man wearing overalls and a black felt hat appeared on the porch.

"Call off yer dogs, Jeb!" Mr. Pentland yelled out. "We ain't a-feelin' to make no dog meat out of ourselves today."

"Git out of the way. Git now!" the man called. Immediately the hounds slunk out of sight around the corner of the cabin.

"Jeb Spencer, this here's Miz Christy Huddleston. New teacher from over Asheville way. Arrived yesterday on the train at El Pano."

"Howdy do, ma'am."

The man had not shaved in days. His beard was growing out blond. He led us through the doorway into firelight. I could barely see. The Spencer cabin had no electricity. In the shadows stood a woman and her five children. The scene looked like a picture in an old photograph album.

"C'mon and see the stranger," Jeb Spencer directed. Then he said to me, "This here's my woman Fairlight. And there's John, my oldest, and Zady and Clara, Little Lulu, and my baby boy."

I wondered if these were some of the children I would teach. I smiled at them, but they didn't move. I was struck by their stringy hair and the dirt smears covering their faces. I held out my hand to Mrs. Spencer who shyly touched my fingers. "Would you like to set a spell?" She pointed to a rickety wooden chair near the fireplace.

My eyes were adjusting to the dim light and as I held my cold hands close to the fire, I looked around. The primitive cabin had only two rooms and one high window to the right of the fireplace. There was no bathroom or indoor plumbing and no rugs on the wooden floor. A narrow ladder led to a hole in the ceiling, probably a loft. A worn saddle, skirts, and tattered pants hung from pegs in the walls. A long-barrelled rifle was laid across an elkhorn rack, and strings of dried onions and red peppers hung from the rafters.

I watched Mrs. Spencer set a pot of steaming cabbage in the middle of a wooden plank table. The mountain woman was tall with black hair parted in the middle and drawn back into a bun. Despite the cold temperature inside the cabin, both she and her children were barefooted. I noticed the children staring at my red sweater and had the feeling they had never seen anything like it.

Before long, everyone gathered around the table. Jeb prayed in a loud voice. "Thank Thee, Lord, for providing this bounty. Bless us and bind us. Amen."

The children scrambled for the tin plates. There were no napkins on the table, and not one person had washed his hands. Mrs. Spencer handed me a chipped pottery plate. I could not help but think about our beautiful china and solid oak dining room table back home.

Suddenly, a squealing pig darted through the open door and jumped on the oldest daughter's lap. "This here's Belinda, our pet pig," Clara explained as she handed the animal a piece of cornbread.

As I sat there, I had the strangest feeling. I felt like I had passed back through time and by some magic, Daniel Boone or Davy Crockett might walk in any moment. This place belonged on the American frontier, not here in Tennessee in 1912. Was I still Christy Rudd Huddleston from Asheville, North Carolina? I wondered what lay ahead for me in this odd, new world I had just entered.

My thoughts were abruptly shattered by a man rushing into the cabin. He leaned against the chimney, out of breath.

"An accident," he gasped. "It's Bob Allen. Hurt bad. A fallin' tree hit him on the head." The man took a deep breath. "They're carryin' him here. He was a-goin' to El Pano to fetch the new teacher."

Within minutes, two men carried a man with a bloody head into the Spencer cabin. They laid him on the old post-and-spindle bed.

"What all happened?" Mr. Pentland asked.

"We was huntin' squirrels when we found him," one of the men began. "Our old hound dog nosed him out. A big tulip poplar tree got wind-throwed and thumped him right on the head."

Outside I heard the stomping of feet and the whinny of a horse. When the door opened, a rugged man with wavy, dark red hair walked in.

"That's Dr. Neil MacNeill," Mr. Pentland whispered at my side. "He's the only doctor in the Cove, this small valley back here in the mountains. Lives over near Big Spoon Creek."

Before long, the strangest group of people I had ever seen were crowded into the Spencer cabin. Mr. Pentland told me they were friends and relatives of the Spencers. I wondered how news could travel so fast in a place with no telephones.

"Mary Allen, I'm needing to talk to you," the doctor ordered when he had finished examining the patient.

An upset woman with hair that hadn't been combed and deep lines in her face pushed forward.

"Mary, I'd best speak plain. Bob's bad off." The doctor's voice was soft and his hazel eyes tender. "There's some bleeding inside his skull. If we leave him like this, he'll die."

Mary Allen rocked on the heels of her untied, water-stained boots. Her eyes stared straight ahead.

"There is one chance, though. I could bore a small hole in the skull to let the bad blood out and try to lift the pressure. But Mary, I've never tried this operation before. I've only watched one. It's risky."

"We've no cause to let go so long as there's one livin' breath left in him." The woman spoke slowly, with a voice like granite. "Would ya try, Doc? We've got six young'uns."

Dr. MacNeill hesitated. I understood the problem. He would be operating in a cabin full of germs, with no nurses and no light. If Mr. Allen died, some of these people would blame him.

"We'll go ahead," he finally announced. "We'll use that kitchen table. Fairlight, will you clear it off? And Jeb, I'll need a razor and hammer. Ben Pentland, didn't I see you here? Take the men down to the spring and get water. We're going to need lots of boiling water.

"Now, the whole kit and caboodle of you had best leave." The doctor spoke gruffly to the rest of us.

Some of the men lifted the patient onto the table. Suddenly, Mary Allen rushed in through the doorway with an axe in her hands. She lifted it over her shoulder and heaved it into the floorboard under the table. Then, she tied a string around one of her husband's wrists.

I was too stunned to move. To my surprise, Dr. MacNeill took this wild behavior calmly. "All right, Mary. That's fine," he said quietly. "There's nothing more you can do for Bob now."

Calmly the doctor sharpened the razor and began to shave the man's head. I escaped outside. I breathed deeply, letting the cold air dilute the sickly smell of ether in the cabin. I felt bad because Mr. Allen had been hurt coming to fetch me. One of the hounds came up and nibbled my hand. I patted the little dog's head.

What am I doing in a place like this? Questions took over my thoughts. *Is this really where I want to be? Should I have listened to my parents' warnings that nineteen is too young to leave home and go to a mountain cove no one has ever seen?*

A long time passed. Finally a voice spoke from the shadows. It was my friend, Mr. Pentland. "You must be tired. Why don't I take you on to the mission now? It's not far."

"But Mr. Allen. How is he?"

"Still livin' and breathin'," he announced. "The doc says he has a fightin' chance."

"I'm so glad," I said with relief.

Mr. Pentland picked up my suitcase, and I followed him. If he delivered any more mail, I didn't remember it. By the time we reached the mission house at Cutter Gap that night, I was too tired to remember anything except someone showing me my room. Soon, I was in bed listening only to the gurgle of a mountain stream flowing outside my bedroom window.

3

My room at the mission house was plain and simple. Two straight chairs sat beside a washstand with a white china pitcher and bowl. On one wall stood an old dresser with a cracked mirror. White net curtains hung at the two windows while two cotton rag rugs covered the bare wood floor.

Curious to see Cutter Gap, I slid out of bed late the next morning and hobbled over to one of the windows. My body was sore from yesterday's walk. Mountain ranges folded one behind the other. In the foreground everything was covered with fresh January snow. Behind that, patches of emerald green shone through. On the smoky blue of the far summits, fluffy white clouds rested like wisps of cotton. I counted eleven mountain peaks rising up and up toward the sky. A smoky blue haze colored everything. Now I understood why these mountains were called the Great Smokies.

I gazed at the summits and took a deep breath. *It's so beautiful!*

A loud knock at my door startled me. A woman with silver hair and a nose too large for her narrow face stood at my door. "I'm Ida Grantland, David's sister," she said, sucking in her thin lower lip. "Would you like some breakfast? Everybody else has eaten."

Miss Ida was a plain woman whose thin grey hair was tied into a tiny bun. I could see some of her scalp. She told me she had come to Cutter Gap to keep house for her brother. At first I had a hard time understanding her because she talked so fast. While she fluttered around the kitchen, she served me hot oatmeal followed by buckwheat cakes and maple syrup. "David's at Low Gap School," she explained as I ate. "Had to leave early this morning. He said to tell you he was sorry not to be here when you woke up."

"I'm sorry I overslept. Does Mr. Grantland teach at the Low Gap School?"

"Oh, no, that school's closed. There were some old desks there they said we could use in the new one." She pointed out the window to a small unfinished building. "David can build anything he sets his hand to. He's working on the steeple now."

"Will that be the school and church both?"

"That's right. You'll hold classes during the week, and David will conduct services each Sunday. We've come a long way in three short months but there's still a lot of work to do. That's David's bunkhouse down by the creek. He sleeps there and takes his meals here."

"Whose cabin is that behind the spruce trees, with the smoke?" I asked.

"That's Miss Alice's. She lives by herself. She just got back from Big Lick Spring. Went right to the Spencers soon as she heard about the operation. She's catching a wink of sleep now. Said to tell you she'd see you later this afternoon."

Just then the side door banged and David Grantland stood in the kitchen doorway. In long quick strides, the young, handsome preacher crossed the room to me, thrusting out his hand. "Miss Huddleston, great that you're here." He had black hair and fine, white, even teeth. His friendly brown eyes were set wide apart. "Not much of a welcome yesterday, was it? Snowstorm, injured man, total confusion."

The preacher stopped at the table to take a few sips of hot coffee. Then he was off. "Got to get another load of school desks and benches while I've got the help. I'll see you later on, after your visit with Miss Alice."

Compared to the Spencer cabin, the mission house was a palace, but it was still rustic. It had no electricity, no telephones, and no plumbing. The house was a white frame, three-story building with a screened porch on each side. Directly behind it loomed a mountain, its base within a few feet of the back door. The house, together with the church-schoolhouse, Mr. Grantland's bunkhouse, Miss Alice's cabin, a springhouse, and an outhouse, made up the mission in Cutter Gap. It was now my home.

That afternoon, I knocked at Miss Alice's door. A tall woman wearing a straight, blue wool skirt and a white linen shirtwaist opened the door.

"Please come in," she said. "Let me hang up your coat. Come over by the fire. Down to ten above zero this morning."

I realized at once that I had to get to know this person. Only someone special could have created a cabin this beautiful in the middle of the dirt and poverty of the Cove. It was warm and colorful and shiny inside her place. Firelight gleamed on polished brass and reflected from a clean, waxed floor. Old pine and cherry furniture was covered by red and blue materials. Windows across the back of the room let in the great outdoors, making the towering mountain peaks look like a gigantic mural.

"Does my cabin surprise you?" she asked.

"I'm sorry. I didn't mean to stare. The place I saw yesterday was so plain and dirty. But this cabin is so clean and beautiful I want to hug it. It's like, well, like coming home."

"That's the nicest compliment my cabin's ever had. Here, sit in this red wing chair. And please, call me Miss Alice."

Mr. Pentland had been right. She was different. There was something queenlike about her. Her once blond hair was now sprinkled with grey, and she wore it braided into a bun, like a crown. She smiled and looked at me with the kindness of a mother.

"Miss Alice, how is Mr. Allen?" I asked as I sat down.

"He opened his eyes about seven this morning. I think he's going to be fine."

Miss Alice sat in an old straight back chair on a flowered cushion. Her next question surprised me. "Tell me, Miss Huddleston, why did you come to Cutter Gap?"

"I thought Dr. Ferrand told you," I answered. "I heard him lecture last summer at a church conference at Montreat near Asheville. He told us about the mountain people. He explained that you needed people who were willing to give more than just money. I volunteered to teach school."

"Dr. Ferrand is a great man," she answered calmly, smoothing out a crease in her skirt, "but he didn't tell me very much about you. Looking back, do you think you were swept away by his words?"

"I suppose I could have been," I hesitated, "but I've had four months to think about it. Dr. Ferrand made it sound as if you needed teachers. I've had a year and a semester of junior college. And I want my life to count for something. You know, more than just staying home."

A quiet, peaceful silence filled the room. My thoughts floated back to my life in Asheville, my parents, our house, my friends. It wasn't that my life in Asheville was bad. It simply wasn't enough. There had to be more to life than shopping and picnics, and I had to find out what it was.

Miss Henderson broke into my thoughts. "So it seemed to you that teaching school here was the next step in making your life count?"

"Yes."

"Then you'll need some facts about your new job," she said brightly. "School opens Monday next. We now have three on staff—you, me, and David."

"How long have you been here, Miss Alice?"

"I first came to the Great Smokies nine years ago. My first school was at Big Lick Springs. Two years later, Cataleechie School got started. Later, some of the families here begged me to come and give their children a better school. A year ago, Dr. Ferrand asked me to work with him here. I would teach and he would travel and tell people about the need."

"And then you built this cabin?"

"Yes, I wanted a quiet place for me and for others who visit me. You see, the people here come from a religious background of fears and taboos. They think that God is a God of rules. You can't do this. You musn't do that. If you do, you'll go to hell.

"I grew up as a Quaker in Pennsylvania. My father was strict, but he gave me one very important thing—a happy childhood. He didn't want me to grow up believing in a God who was mean. He wanted me to know God as love." Miss Alice sighed. "We need to show these folks a God who can give them joy. They need joy. They lead such hard lives . . ." Her voice trailed off.

"I'm afraid poverty is all I've seen so far," I chimed in.

She nodded. "At first, I couldn't see behind the dirt either. Yet as I rode through the mountains and came to know the people, something else happened. I started seeing beyond their broken-down shanties and dirty faces. It was like looking through a tiny peephole in a big wall.

"These mountain people are rich in heritage. Their ancestors settled here from Scotland and Ireland. Many of them have royal blood flowing through their veins. They have good, sharp minds, but back here in these hills they haven't had much of a chance to use them. They are loyal and extremely independent. But all of this comes at great cost. Their iron will keeps them living a life of feuds."

"You mean they shoot and kill one another?" I asked in shock.

For the first time Miss Alice's face turned grim. "We've had a great deal of violence," she began.

The room was quiet as she told me of these proud people, their Scotch-Irish background, and the feuds. With surprise I realized two hours had passed. As I rose to go, Miss Alice held out her hand to me. "Christy Huddleston, I think thee will do."

Miss Alice had slipped into her Quaker speech. The warmth in her voice and her soothing words made me feel glad to be in Cutter Gap.

4

"Is this a fashion parade on Fifth Avenue?" It was the first day of school, and David's voice was teasing. I was picking my way along the cleaned walk from the mission house to the school in my dainty heels. David kept pace beside me in the deep snow. He wore heavy boots laced almost to his knees. "Hold on! Steady!" he exclaimed as I slipped and he reached out to support me.

When we finally reached the unfinished schoolhouse, the yard was swarming with children waiting for their first look at the new teacher. They were climbing over the piles of lumber and rocks in the yard. Some were running in and out of the building, squealing and yelling in the clear air. Most of them were very skinny and very pale. None were dressed warmly enough for the cold January morning.

"The children are excited," David said.

Seeing us coming, the children stopped what they were doing to stare at me. As we got closer, I noticed that many

29

of them were barefooted. I was shocked. Some had walked several miles in the snow to reach the mission. Suddenly I was painfully self-conscious about my foolish shoes. The children's bare feet made me want to tuck my own feet out of sight. What a lot I had to learn!

At that moment a little boy with carrot-red hair came running up to us. His eyes were the deepest blue. "Teacher, I've come to see you and to swap howdys," he said in almost musical rhythm. "I memorized your name. It's shore a funny name. I never heerd a name like it a'fore."

"Miss Huddleston," David said solemnly, "this is Little Burl Allen, one of Bob Allen's sons."

All over again, I felt grateful for the good news about Mr. Allen. I reached down for the little hand. It was cold. "I'm delighted to swap howdys with you, Little Burl."

As David and I climbed the steps to the school, I whispered, "At least we could do something about their bare feet. It's shameful."

David's brown eyes crinkled at the corners. "I know it's a shock. But up in these mountains, the youngsters have gone barefooted all their lives—summer and winter."

The schoolroom smelled of varnish and wood smoke and cedar pencils and chalk. I stood beside the battered secondhand teacher's desk and surveyed the situation. The girls had seated themselves on one side and the boys on the other. I later learned this was part of a centuries-old tradition brought over from Scotland and Ireland. Several of the pupils seemed older than I, and some were tiny, not more than five years old. I recognized four of the Spencer children and nodded to them.

As David introduced me, I tried to count the number of children in the room. I counted the number of desks in each row—nine; then number of rows—eight; seventy-two, with five desks empty. Oh my! How could one teacher handle sixty-seven children?

"Thank you, Mr. Grantland. I—I'm glad to be here. And now," I said looking directly at him, "I know that you have all sorts of things to do, so we won't ask you to stay." I couldn't bear the thought of him watching my first fumbling attempt at teaching. He was only seven years older than I but he seemed a thousand years older in experience.

David whispered, "Sure you don't want me to stay?" For a moment, I was not sure, especially when I noticed how closely he watched some big boys at the back of the room.

"Lundy Taylor . . ." With a low voice, David addressed one of the boys who sat with his arms folded defiantly across his chest. The boy was as large as a grown man, with a red pimply neck and a face that could have used a shave. "He's never been to school before with Allen children," David added.

I didn't know what that meant. But I did know that Miss Alice had already warned me to stake my ground the first day.

"I'll be fine. You go ahead," I said firmly.

David left and I took a deep breath. I was on my own. All of a sudden the children seemed like giants. I leaned against the edge of the desk for support and remembered that Tennessee law required us to start the day with prayer. Miss Alice had been right. I needed all the prayer I could get.

I held up one hand and asked the children to bow their heads. Trying to keep my voice steady, I prayed: "We thank Thee for those who cared enough to fix up this beautiful new school for us. Be with us as we begin. Amen."

After the children had joined in some boisterous mountain songs, I started to take roll. I walked over to a row of boys. "What's your name?"

"Front name or back name?"

"Well—er—both."

"Front name be Sam Houston."

"A fine name," I replied. "Sam Houston was a Tennessee hero. Well now, what is your—er—back name?"

"Holcombe, ma'am. I be nine years old. I never been to school a'fore."

"Oh, well, I think you're going to like it." I hesitated then pushed on. "So tell me, Sam Houston, what is your address? Tell me where you live."

"Well—" The boy's small face looked puzzled. "First ye cross Cutter Branch. Then ye cut across Lonesome Pine Ridge. At the third fork in the trail, ye scoot under the fence and head for Pigeonroost Hollow. Then ye spy our cabin and pull into our place, 'bout two mile or so from the Spencers."

I could see I was going to have to come up with another system for getting addresses in Cutter Gap. "Thank you, Sam."

"Generally go by Sam Houston, Teacher."

"All right, Sam Houston." I smiled and turned toward the next boy in the row. "And what is your front name?"

The youngster quickly replied, "Front name be Zacharias. Back name be Holt. Zacharias Jehoshaphat Holt."

The boy sitting behind him said softly, "Plumb crazy. Ain't yer name a-tall."

"This isn't the time for fooling," I replied with authority. "We're trying to get the roll down. Now tell me your real name."

"Zacharias Jehoshaphat—" With that his right ear jerked violently. The children roared with laughter. Some of them even doubled over. Only the boy who had spoken up kept a straight face. "Teacher, that's not his name. He be a-packin' lies. You can tell. Jest look at his ear."

Sure enough, Zacharias's ear jerked again. "Certainly, I see his ear, but what's that got to do with not telling the truth?"

"Oh, ma'am, all them Holts when they tell a whopper, their ears twitch."

I turned to the boy again. "Tell me your name."

Once again, the ear wiggled. But now I saw it—a string over the ear! I reached to remove the cord, but the boy behind jerked it away from me and stuffed the string in his desk. I marched to the desk and reached in, only to have my fingers meet a mass of wriggling fur.

"Eeee!" I squealed, stepping backwards. A ring-tailed raccoon clambered onto the desk screeching. It sat there looking at me from behind its funny masked face, clenching one end of the string in its teeth.

By now, the schoolroom was bedlam with whooping and hollering. I looked at the boy who'd had the string on his ear.

"Creed thar put me up to it. Said if'n I'd do it, he'd let me sleep with his coon for one night."

The boy with the raccoon looked just like Tom Sawyer. He wore overalls, had lots of freckles and two missing front teeth. "What's your name? Creed what?"

"Creed Josiah Allen," he smirked.

My heart softened. This was another Allen child. "This is your raccoon, Creed?"

"Yes'm. My pet coon, Scalawag. Got him from a kit last summer."

"What's a kit?"

"Like a nest. He's most grown now. Sleeps with me. He be clean though. Coons wash everything a'fore they eat."

"I've heard that."

"Coons are the main best pets in the world," he spoke with certainty. "If ye'd like one fer yerself, Teacher, come spring, maybe we'uns could spy out a kit and git one for ye."

"Uh, thanks, Creed. Let me think about that offer. Now about Scalawag and school."

"Oh, Scalawag won't cause no trouble. Cross my heart and hope to die."

What could I say? I didn't want to ruin this relationship before it got started. Suddenly I had an inspiration. I crouched down and lowered my voice. "It's like this, Creed, just between you and me. Promise you won't tell."

"Cross my heart."

"Scalawag is such a fine coon, you know so good-looking and such an actor, that the children will want to watch

34

him instead of doing their lessons. Let's make a pact. You leave Scalawag home after this, and I'll let you bring him to the last social just before school closes. We'll fix it so that Scalawag will be part of the entertainment."

"Honest, Teacher!" His face was shining. "That be a sealed bargain, fair and square. Land o' livin'! Put it thar, Teacher!" He stuck out a grubby hand.

Although taking the roll was different from what I had expected, it became very valuable to me. The children volunteered all sorts of information on the side. I discovered that John Spencer, fifteen, had worked all the figures in a battered old geometry book on his desk, and he wanted a harder book. I also learned that most of the children had never been to school before and were eager to learn.

Finally came our noon recess. The children called it "the dinner spell." Even before they opened their dinner pails, some of the children had organized a singing game. How they loved to sing. Their voices filled the crisp, cold air.

Here come five dukes, a-rovin', a-rovin',
    a-rovin',
Here come five dukes a-rovin', with a heigh
    a-ransomtee.
We're quite as good as you sires, one of us, sires, one
    of us, sires,
Pray will you have one of us sires, with a heigh
    a-ransomtee.

The song sounded so British. The children were singing songs from their heritage, just as Miss Alice had said. Imagine, songs about dukes and sires in the backwoods hills of Tennessee!

I stood at the doorway listening. Suddenly, a screech of pain shattered the hum of their voices. I ran down the steps to find five-year-old Vella Holt crumpled up on the ground, sobbing. The other children had gathered in a circle around her.

"Vella's got a knot on her head," a voice volunteered as I took the little girl with auburn pigtails in my arms. She stared up at me with the biggest brown eyes I had ever seen.

Zacharias's little sister did have a large bump. What was worse, the blow had been dangerously close to the side of her temple.

"What happened?" I asked.

No one answered. I looked up. "Did Vella fall down?"

"No ma'am," someone said softly. "She got hit."

"How?"

Another child thrust a homemade ball into my hands. It was so heavy I almost dropped it. The ball was made of strips of old cloth wound round and round and bound with thread. When I pushed a thumb through the cloth, I found a rock at the center.

"Vella got hit with this? Who threw it?"

Again, silence. Then out of the corner of my eye I spied Lundy Taylor slinking into the empty schoolhouse.

"Did Lundy throw this?" The children didn't answer, but their eyes told me the truth. I felt chilled and frightened. What sort of boy would do such a thing and why?

5

It was now February, and I
had been teaching school in
Cutter Gap for almost a
month. After the
first couple of weeks,
I had thought things
would get easier. How
wrong I was! My troubles
were multiplying faster
than the freckles on Creed
Allen's face!

For one thing, many of the children came to school
hungry and couldn't concentrate. In addition to their
drippy noses, I realized that a number of them had eye
problems because they squinted and kept shielding
their eyes from the light. I wasn't making much progress
in my teaching either. I had tried to divide the children
by grades, but the children would not cooperate. "No
ma'am, I can't sit by no boy," the girls would say over

and over. "This ain't a courtin' school. My paw'll take me out if'n ye make it a courtin' school." And of course, the children had to learn Latin before anything else. Their parents insisted on it. It had been taught in the Old Country and any boy or girl without Latin "didn't have no learnin' a-tall."

And then there were the smells. The schoolroom reeked with horrible odors. The children stayed dirty because they never bathed. My nose had a terrible time. I tried to keep the windows open as much as possible, but that didn't help. So I decided to saturate my handkerchief with perfume and pull it from my sleeve to dab my nose. I hoped the children wouldn't notice.

In desperation, I prayed, "Oh, God, this isn't funny. Please change my nose or help me get the children cleaned up in a hurry!"

One day, I thought of including a health lesson in our studies. We talked about the skin and the necessity of washing. When it came to bathing though, I had trouble. The families in the Cove had no indoor plumbing. They used a granite tub or a pan in front of an open fire. And that was not easy with six or eight people living in a one- or two-room cabin. I talked with the children about pure drinking water and the dangers of typhoid and discovered how often they went to the bathroom in the mountain streams. We had a long way to go.

Besides all this, there were the pigs. In the Cove most of them weren't penned so they wandered at will, fattening themselves on beechnuts and acorns. Some slept right under the new schoolhouse, and they grunted and snorted so loudly I could barely teach. I didn't know what to do.

Another problem was Mountie O'Teale. She was ten years old yet she never laughed or even smiled. When she tried to speak, the youngster stuttered or grunted like an animal, and the children teased her.

One afternoon, I caught Creed Allen mistreating her. He had bent a sycamore twig into a bow then released it to hit her in the face. When she started crying, the prankster chanted:

> Mush-mouthed Mountie,
> Can't even speak,
> Jabber jabber jaybird
> Marbles in the beak.

"Look at her blubber," he taunted. "I dare you to blab to Teacher."

Misery poured out of Mountie's big brown eyes. I knew I had to find a way to reach behind the wall of hurt she had built up. Later, as I was standing at my bedroom window, a thought came to me: *Watch for an opportunity to do something special for Mountie, something that will please her.*

That chance came the next day. For the first time, I noticed she wore a shabby coat with no buttons. While the students were outside for recess, I sewed on some large buttons and carefully hung her coat back on its peg. After school, I heard a giggle at the back of the room. I looked up to see Mountie.

"Mountie, what's so funny?"

The child bounced up to my desk, pointed to the buttons on her coat and exclaimed, "Look at my buttons! Look at my buttons!"

"Mountie, what did you say?"

"Teacher, look! See my pretty buttons!"

I could scarcely believe my ears. The child was speaking plainly for the first time. I was watching a miracle right before my eyes.

That night a second clear thought came to me about Mountie's speech problem. *Maybe what she needs is to know that someone loves her.* I decided to give her a gift.

The next day after school, I presented her with a red scarf my mother had knitted me. "Mountie, I want you to have this. It's a special gift from me to you," I told her as I handed her the scarf. Mountie's eyes lit up. She hugged me over and over and danced down the schoolroom aisle waving the scarf.

With every bit of encouragement, the ten-year-old grew more secure. And she began to make amazing progress in both her speech and her reading. I had learned a very valuable lesson. What these children needed most was love, and this love could work miracles.

But many of the children, like Lundy, were hard to love. I told myself I did not have to love everyone. Little Burl showed me I was wrong.

One morning, we interrupted our spelling lesson to watch the birds at our school feeding station. It was early March, and a variety of birds were appearing. My pupils were fascinated. This particular morning, we had already seen several juncos and some titmice. Now a pair of colorful cardinals were stuffing themselves on the crumbs and sunflower seeds.

"Isn't it great how many different kinds of birds there are!" I told my pupils as we admired the brilliant red feathers. "God must have cared about them, or He wouldn't have made them so beautiful. You know, children, He loves everything He's made—every bird, every animal, and every single one of you. He loves you extra specially."

As my students returned to their desks, I noticed Little Burl. He was sitting at his desk staring at the rafters, his red cowlick sticking straight up. The youngster's face was puckered into a look of deep thought.

All at once, he jumped up, ran up to my desk, and wrapped his two little arms around my neck in a hug. "Teacher, Teacher," he said, stretching his neck up to look me full in the eyes. "Ain't it true, Teacher, that if God loves everbody, then we'uns got to love everbody too?"

I looked at the six-year-old in amazement. "Yes, Little Burl, it's true. Forever and forever."

At that moment, I shut down my privilege of disliking anyone I chose. A growing compassion began to fill my heart. And gradually the smells in the schoolroom no longer seemed so bad. It was not that the hygiene lessons had made a difference or that my nose had grown less sensitive. It was that I was coming to know the children at Cutter Gap as people rather than names in my gradebook. I was letting love come in the front door while my nose crept out the back. I was learning, too.

6

From upstairs in my room, I heard banging on the front door, late one Saturday afternoon in March. I rushed down to find Ruby Mae Morrison on the porch. Ruby Mae was staying at the mission for awhile. Her stepfather had kicked her out in a fit of anger, so Miss Alice had offered the fifteen-year-old a place with us. She attended the mission school.

"Teacher, I was visitin' the McHones. The baby quit breathin' last night. Miz McHone's carryin' on right bad." Ruby Mae tossed her tangled red hair out of her face. "This was the only gal-baby followin' a passel of three boys. Miz Henderson's over Big Lick Spring way. She wants you to come, Miz Christy, and holp her fix up the least'un real purty. I can show you the way."

"Of course, I'll come," I replied quickly. "Let me gather some things."

43

I rushed back upstairs to look for some soap, clean rags, and safety pins. I grabbed some ribbons from my dresser and found a baby dress in the mission's used clothing box. I placed everything in a basket, and we were off.

When I first arrived at the mission Ruby Mae's constant chattering, like a squirrel, had made me mad. But Miss Alice had told me that God often uses things that bother us to bless us. So I began to thank God for Ruby Mae and soon realized that her talking was an opportunity to understand more about the mountain people. Today, her coming to get me was her way of reaching out to help someone in need.

At last we reached the edge of a clearing at the foot of Big Butt Knob beyond Coldsprings Branch. A rickety log cabin stood in the horseshoe bend of a wide bubbling creek. It had been built on stilts and like all the mountain homes had never been painted. The yard was muddy from the melting snow. Huge bare red spruce trees towered nearby.

"Hello! It's us—Ruby Mae and Teacher," Ruby Mae yelled.

Almost at once, a skinny woman with brown straggly hair appeared on the porch. She was young and wore a wrinkled skirt with an old blue sweater buttoned loosely over her stomach. Her feet were in a pair of men's shoes.

"Thank ya for comin'. The baby cried something awful all night. We thought it was liver-growed," she explained as she took us inside.

"Mrs. McHone, I never heard of that. What's liver-grown?" I asked.

44

"Lots of newborn babies has it. You take the baby by the left heel and the right hand and make them touch. Then you does the same with the left hand and right heel. If they don't touch, the baby's liver-growed. So you gots to force the hand and heel to touch. I tried, but the baby hollered and went limp. Never could do nothin' after that. Weren't no time to call Doc MacNeill."

The mother was crying and wiping her eyes with the hem of a stained apron that had been hanging on a nearby chair. My heart almost broke in two. Opal McHone had injured her own baby without even knowing it, and that injury had caused the baby's death.

I turned for a moment to the three McHone boys standing in one corner of the room in the shadows. Toot and Vincent were still so young. They attended the mission school, along with Isaak, the oldest son. My heart warmed as I looked at the twelve-year-old wearing his usual raggedy, patched overalls and heavy workshoes. His sad brown eyes met mine.

The father, Tom McHone, stepped forward to shake my hand. Then an older man named Uncle Bogg, Tom's father, added, "Howdy do, Miss. Mighty proud that you dropped in." Ruby Mae had told me about this man. Everybody in the Cove called him Uncle Bogg because he was so well loved. He was known for his tall tales and stories about mountain life. The grandfather's head was bald and shiny. He had a wrinkled forehead, and long, curly, grey fluff grew over his ears. He smiled at me with a toothless grin. "Let me holp you if I can," he offered. "I can git you some water."

Ruby Mae helped me dress the baby for burial. All the while, Opal sat by the fireplace staring ahead. "Can't thank ye enough for comin'," she repeated over and over like a chorus in a hymn. "Don't know how's I would've done this without you, Miss Christy."

"I'm so sorry this has happened." I tried to find words of comfort, all the while wondering why the doctor wasn't teaching mothers how to care for their newborn babies. These people needed to learn.

"Why, Miz Christy," Opal exclaimed after we had finished. "My baby looks plumb purty. No baby in the Cove has ever had ribbons a'fore. I'm obleeged to you!"

"Glad I could help," I stammered. "Maybe you'll have another baby girl someday."

Uncle Bogg stepped forward. "I'll git the lantern and see the two of you home," he offered.

"Ruby Mae knows the way back," I began.

"No use arguin'. It's nigh dark, and I'm a'goin' with you."

The old man picked up a kerosene lantern and his rifle and was soon leading us back. Dry leaves and twigs crunched underfoot. All around us red squirrels and grouse chattered in the twilight. Suddenly, a twig snapped loudly in the woods to our left. We all jumped. The old man stopped instantly, set the lantern down and positioned his right hand on the trigger of his gun.

"Thought I heerd a varmint," he explained after a long silence.

Somehow that explanation did not convince me. Why would wild animals make a mountain man so jittery? Ruby Mae's face looked chalky white in the dim light.

"Thought I seen a shadder movin'. There!" she whispered, pointing into the woods.

Uncle Bogg raised the lantern and peered. "Lots of shadders," he answered. "C'mon, let's go."

After that, he quickened his pace but clutched his gun in his right hand. Ruby Mae and I had trouble keeping up with him.

By now the moon had risen, and everything was bathed in its soft light. At last, we reached the edge of the mission yard.

"Am I glad to see you!" David exclaimed rushing up to greet us. "Uncle Bogg, thanks for walking the girls home."

The old man spit a stream of tobacco juice. "Opal's baby died last night, Preacher. She asked Miz Christy to come and holp."

"Ida has waited supper for you. You'd better go on in and eat," David directed.

Ruby Mae and I walked toward the house, while David leaned on the fence to talk with Uncle Bogg. I couldn't hear what they said.

Later that evening, Miss Alice stopped by my bedroom and sat on the edge of the bed beside me.

"Maybe my parents were right," I sobbed. "I don't belong here. Babies die because mothers are ignorant. The children don't bathe, and they're so poor they don't even have clothes that fit. I don't know what to do. I shouldn't have come."

Miss Alice patted my hand. Her hands were large but her touch was tender. "Maybe it's just as well this happened. Now is as good a time as any to decide whether you'll stay or go home."

"Not much of life can be as bad as what I saw tonight." I blew my nose in my white handkerchief.

"It's hard to look honestly at the way life really is, Christy," she said kindly. "A lot of life is ugly. You're not the only one who has ever wanted to run away.

"You're sensitive, my child, and that's all right. But God doesn't use fragile china dolls that break easily. He needs people who will face the suffering and permit Him to change it through them."

"But if God is so loving, why doesn't He stop the bad things from happening?" The bitter question clawed at my throat. "Why, Miss Alice?"

In her usual quiet way, Miss Alice remained silent for a moment. This gentle woman had a beauty I wanted. It was the beauty of peace. Somehow Miss Alice had come to terms with life. She knew where she belonged and what she should be doing. I longed for that same peace. I waited as she arranged the folds of her grey linen skirt on the side of my bed.

"Christy, God has given us two choices in life. We can go His way or we can choose our own. It's up to us," she finally said.

"But how do we go God's way?" I truly wanted to understand.

She tilted her head to one side. I noticed tiny white flowers tucked in her bun. "He gives us very detailed instructions. We find them in His Word. We must love the Lord with all our hearts. We must love our neighbors, and we must be willing to forgive. These aren't easy things to do."

I tossed my long dark hair behind my shoulders and listened.

"Each of us must decide how we're going to live our lives. We can try to tell ourselves evil doesn't exist. We can pretend that someone else's pain is none of our business. Or we can listen for God's orders and walk in faith, believing that He will somehow bring change through us."

"But how?" I propped myself up on my pillows.

"That's the miracle," she replied with a gleam in her eye. "If we decide to follow God, we must open our hearts to the kind of tragedy you saw today. When we do, we begin to see these things differently. We change, and this change makes us realize God's touch in our everyday lives. The Lord can work in others through our love. It's a powerful thing, Christy. This kind of heart love brings miracles."

"So do I go home or stay?" I dared to ask.

She smiled. "Christy Huddleston, who are you?"

"I don't know." My heart sank.

"You can know. Each of us can. God will show you. No one else in the world can fill the place He has designed for you, Christy. No one."

As Miss Alice left that evening, I knew what I had to do, but I didn't know what it would mean. If I was really supposed to stay here, I had to accept the death of babies and the children's bad smells. I had to be the one that changed. And maybe, just maybe, God would use me in some way to help.

Twice each month, David held Sunday school at the Lufty Branch Church. One Sunday afternoon in late March I decided to ride Theo, the mission mule, and go with him.

We rode under a cathedral arch of giant beeches and red spruce. I knew I must look funny riding sidesaddle using a man's tack. My black woolen riding skirt was draped over the mule's belly, almost dragging the ground.

I watched David trotting ahead of me on a new horse, Prince. I smiled to myself when I remembered how we had gotten Prince. During another talk, Miss Alice had suggested I begin to claim some of the promises found in the Bible. At the mission we needed many items in order to do our work properly. One of those was a horse. The Bible says that you have not because you ask not, so I asked God to send us a horse. I realized that horses cost around $100, and we certainly didn't have $100 to spend. But I wanted to stake a claim and see what would happen. Three days after my prayer, a letter had arrived with $106 in it! I knew immediately what the money was for. As we rode to church, my heart leaped for joy. David was riding that answer right in front of me.

Now, we were coming to the deepest part of the woods. The tall tulip trees around me stood like soldiers at attention over a silence that stretched backward into time. These trees had guarded the Cherokee Indians before the arrival of the white man. I imagined myself as one of the first white settlers streaming down the Wilderness Road on horses and covered wagons. I was struck by how slowly time seemed to move in these mountains.

Suddenly, Theo stumbled over a large root in the path. "Are you all right?" David called as he waited for me to catch up.

"I'm fine," I yelled back hoping it wouldn't happen again.

"Christy," David's voice turned serious as Theo and I trotted up, "don't take any more trips away from the mission without me."

"Why?" I stared at him. "What's the matter?"

"I'm not sure," he replied. "The other night on your way back from the McHone cabin, Uncle Bogg saw some men following you. He'd never seen them before, and Uncle Bogg knows every man, woman, and puppy dog between here and the North Carolina line."

"What would strangers be doing in Cutter Gap?"

"That's what I want to know," he stated firmly, creasing his brow. "And I intend to find out."

Soon we could hear the sound of rushing water ahead. Big Spoon Creek plunged down the mountain across our path. David halted on the bank. With frozen edges, the swirling water whipped itself into frothy bubbles as it plunged over the rocks. "The water's higher than I've ever seen it," he said. "I'll go first."

Prince stepped confidently into the water, plunged on into midstream, and splashed up the opposite bank. I gently urged Theo into the creek. Suddenly I felt icy water on my legs.

"David, Theo's falling!" I shrieked.

"Hang on. Stay on his back!"

I clutched the mule's neck to keep from sliding off. "It's his bad hip. I'm too heavy for him."

David shook his head. "It's no use, Christy. Jump off, and I'll help you."

The waist-high water and my heavy wet skirt tugged me downstream. I struggled toward shore. David pulled me up on the bank. "You can't go to Lufty Branch like this. Doc MacNeill's cabin is nearby. Let's stop there."

My teeth chattered as I tried to wring the water out of my skirt. I was freezing. David insisted that I ride Prince while he led Theo up the trail.

"There it is." David pointed to a silvery grey cabin with smoke trailing from the chimney. "That's Doc's place."

Dr. MacNeill came striding down the hill to meet us. Wearing brown corduroys and a plaid hunting shirt, he looked more like a woodsman than a physician. "Anything wrong?"

"Christy got soaked in the creek. Could we dry her out by your fire?"

"Come on up," he replied.

By now my legs were numb with cold and my shoes were stiff. David helped me dismount, and we went inside.

The doctor's cabin smelled of pipe tobacco and burning wood. I immediately noticed stuffed deer heads on the walls and a bearskin rug on the hearth.

He pulled out a three-legged stool for me. "Miss Huddleston, sit down here. Let me see if I can find you something else to wear. We'll dry your clothing here by the fire." The doctor took a key out of his pocket to unlock a closed door to the right of the main room. He went inside and closed the door behind him. I glanced at David who looked as puzzled as I did.

Soon he returned with a flowered dress. "Think you could get into this?" he said as he shut the door and locked it again.

"Yes," I replied thankfully. "It looks like my size."

He led me into a second room to change. It was the doctor's bedroom. I shut the door and looked around. There was a pine four-poster bed with a bedspread hastily pulled up over a huge featherbed and an open cupboard filled with medical books. Quickly I got out of my wet things and into the nice dry dress.

As I opened the door, I heard the doctor say, "It's two-thirty, David."

"We're supposed to be at Lufty Branch by three," he replied. "Ah, Christy, we were just talking about the time. Since I only have thirty minutes until Sunday school, and your skirt won't dry in time for us to make it, I think you should stay here. I'll return for you on my way back."

I felt uncomfortable sitting alone with Dr. MacNeill in his cabin. He seemed so different from the other mountain men. His rugged features made him look like his face had been chiseled out of stone, but his hazel eyes were sensitive and kind. He didn't look like he belonged in the backwoods of Tennessee.

"Drink this," he ordered with a smile, handing me a mug of hot grog. "It's good mountain brew, and it's sure to cure any side effects of your swim in the creek."

I hesitated but realized it was useless to protest. Dr. MacNeill had a forceful way about him. I watched him fill his pipe. Carefully he tapped in the tobacco with hands that were creased and stained.

"You're curious about the dress, I'm sure," he offered quietly. "It belonged to my wife. She died three years ago in childbirth."

"I'm sorry," I replied.

"As for me, I was born in this cabin. My parents and my grandparents were, too. So you see—I'm a hillbilly."

"You don't talk like one."

The doctor puffed on his pipe. "I lapse into mountain talk when I'm with the natives. However, I've had some schooling outside—college, then medical school." He placed two more logs on the fire and turned my skirt over to dry the other side.

"Dr. MacNeill, could you answer some questions for me?" The doctor remained silent. "I'm confused about a few things."

"What?"

"Well, for one thing the McHone baby. It didn't have to die."

The doctor smiled. "Miss Huddleston, Opal Mc-Hone's granny was Scotch-Irish, and Granny's word was gospel when it came to medicine. She believed the super-stition that touching the baby's feet and hands would make it get well. She taught Opal about the liver-grown ailment."

"You mean Mrs. McHone won't listen to you?"

"Not when my word crosses Granny's." The doctor paused to puff on his pipe again.

I continued. "What about Mary Allen? The day of the operation, she heaved an axe into the floor. Why?"

He ran his fingers through his long wavy hair. "Another mountain superstition. An axe is supposed to keep a person from bleeding to death. Mary tied a string around Bob's wrist, too. Remember? That was to keep disease away."

The doctor tapped the ashes out of his pipe on the edge of the fireplace.

"But there's still so much disease," I ventured.

He shrugged as he turned to put another log on the fire. "Yes, there is. When I finished medical school, I decided to return here because these are my people. I knew how desperately they needed a doctor back in these hills. I also realized they couldn't be changed all at once. Time moves more slowly back here, Miss Huddleston. And we've got deeper problems than just superstitions and dirt and smells."

The man picked up a cattail reed from a nearby jug and ran it through his pipe stem. He relit his pipe. "How much do you know about the murders back in these mountains?" he asked through a cloud of smoke.

"Not much. Several people have hinted at them, that's all."

"You don't know the Taylor-Allen story?"

I shook my head.

"In my father's time, the spring of '79 it was, MacKinley Taylor murdered Otis Allen. The dispute involved Coldsprings, one of the best springs in these mountains. Since then, nine men have been killed, three since I've returned to practice medicine."

"Won't the law do anything?"

"No, in the eyes of these mountaineers, courts are unfair. Each family takes care of its own business. Family loyalty comes before everything else. Carrying grudges is a mark of true character in these hills. Back here, grudges go to the grave, and murderers get off." The doctor went on. "The El Pano district has a county squire who's ruled this county for eighteen years. There hasn't been one sentence for murder in all that time."

"Who's the squire?"

"Uncle Bogg."

"You can't be serious!" I was shocked. "He's such a likeable old man."

"I'm quite serious. Uncle Bogg believes that family quarrels are family business, and the courts shouldn't interfere."

"But if the Allens and Taylors are still feuding, what about the children? I'm teaching them in school together."

The doctor sat back in his chair and smiled. "You have no idea what an accomplishment that is. We can thank Miss Alice for that."

The doctor looked at me and chuckled. "Your eyes are very expressive, Miss Huddleston. How long have you been at the mission?"

"A little over two months."

"You've made some strong judgments in these two months, haven't you?"

I could feel my cheeks getting hot. "Are you saying we can't do anything about the health problems until we stop the feuding? It's just that the people will always have disease if they stay dirty."

"And you think my job is to clean them up." The doctor stood up and walked toward the open cabin door to look across the front porch. "I only wish it was that easy. Cleaning up the dirt and smells isn't the real problem. Stopping the hate is."

David returned a short while later. As we left for the mission house, my thoughts focused on what Dr. Mac-Neill had told me. *Can the doctor's Cutter Gap be the same place I heard about that day in Montreat? How much does David know about these murders?*

As we rode home, I asked David, and he answered willingly. "I know enough. I don't want to scare you, but the doctor is right. We must stop the hatred and feuding."

"I can see that's important, but, David, how can a doctor go in and out of these cabins year after year and leave the people as dirty as always?"

"He's a good man, Christy. His ancestors were as distinguished a family as ever came out of Scotland. Their ancestral castle is still there. These are his people, and he wants to help them."

"So how do we stop the feuding?"

The sound of the animals' hooves and their heavy breathing echoed through the giant trees. I could feel the coolness of dusk among the shadows.

"I don't know the answer to that, Christy," David replied as we rode the wide dirt trail side by side. "All I know is that we have to try."

8

"Children, I have a big surprise for you!" I pulled down a large colorful map from its shiny roller case. "I wrote a friend of my father's in Knoxville, a Mr. Smith, and asked him to help us. He has sent us this map and some brand new textbooks."

At last, I had some tools to show my students the world beyond Cutter Gap. Immediately we located Tennessee on the map of the United States. Zacharias Holt stuck a pin with a red paper flag at Cutter Gap.

Next I held up a new textbook from the piles of books on my desk. "He gave us these, too," I proudly announced. The children had never seen books so fresh and clean, with all their covers still there and not a page missing. "We must treat our books like friends, children. So let's have clean hands before we handle them and turn the pages carefully."

We had algebra and geometry books, Latin texts for four years, and many fine literature books. At once John Spencer located the calculus book, looking as if he had been handed a gift of the moon. Rob Allen and Isaak McHone were fascinated with the reading books.

Later that day I read Samuel Taylor Coleridge's "Kubla Khan" from our copy of *English Romantic Poets*. I had no sooner finished than Isaak raised his hand. "Kin I learn it by heart, Teacher? All of it?" When school let out that day, he marched out the door rolling the rhythms over his tongue and reciting to the other children:

> In Xanadu did Kubla Khan
> A stately pleasure-dome decree;
> Where Alph, the sacred river, ran
> Through caverns measureless to man
> Down to a sunless sea . . .

One Friday morning in early April I headed for the schoolhouse to prepare for the end-of-the-week spelling bee. While crossing the yard, I spied papers littering the ground and the schoolhouse door ajar. I quickened my steps.

As I pushed the door open, I drew in my breath. The room was wrecked. I ran toward the front. Someone had thrown the books wildly around my desk. They had ripped out pages, wadded them up, and even slashed some.

Our beautiful new books! Anger screamed inside me. *Why? Is someone mad at the mission?* I remembered little Vella Holt the day she'd been hit with the hidden rock. This was the same kind of prank—vicious and senseless.

I looked up. *Oh, no!* Two of our new maps had been drawn down out of their cases and slashed with a knife. Weak-kneed, I sank into the nearest seat to stare at the destruction before me.

The children and I spent much of the morning putting torn books and maps back together as best we could. We matched pieces, mending and pasting.

As I started to write the spelling-bee list on the board, I noticed how chilly the room was. Today's skies were cloudy and a cold wind had blown up. I walked over to open the iron grating in our potbellied stove and poke up the fire. Sparks and flames spat into my face. A series of explosions shattered the air. I cried out as I slapped at the burning pieces in my hair and on my dress.

The room was deathly silent. Some of the children wouldn't even look at me. Finally Clara Spencer spoke up, "Hit be buckeyes, ma'am. Buckeyes in the ashes. They git hot and then pop and fly all to pieces when the air hits 'em."

I wanted to run away and never come back. "I bragged about you in my letters to Mr. Smith," I wailed. "I told him you were different from boys and girls in other schools. I told him how proud I was of you—that there had never been students so eager to learn. What do I tell him now? That I was wrong?"

I bit my lip, choking back the words, and whirled around toward the blackboard to get on with writing the spelling words. I had only written a few when a steady noise at the back penetrated my tortured thoughts. "He-hee . . . He-hee." I whipped around just in time to catch

63

Lundy stalking down the aisle, poking a stick into Mountie O'Teale's back.

"Lundy," I forced myself to stay calm. "Stop talking and get back to your seat."

The huge boy stood there gawking at me with fire in his eyes. "No gal-woman's goin' to tell me what to do," he snarled. "I'll stop when I'm good and ready."

With a courage I did not know I had, I stormed down the aisle toward the sneering face. The fact that the boy towered at least a head above me did not matter.

"You'll stop when I tell you to," I ordered, "and I'm telling you—right—now." Then I reached up and grabbed a shock of his dark matted hair, dragged him down the aisle and shook him as I shoved him into the nearest seat.

The yank took Lundy by surprise. His pale blue eyes blinked back tears. But the next moment he was standing up, his fists doubled as if to fight me back. By now, most of the children were on their feet.

"Lundy—stay—right—there!" David's stern masculine voice roared from the open doorway. "One more word out of you, and I'm the one you'll fight."

I had never been so glad to see anyone in my whole life. The boy slunk down immediately. The crisis was over—for the moment.

After supper that evening, Miss Alice, David, and I chatted by the fireplace.

"But I lost my temper and yelled at the children. Then I yanked Lundy by the hair . . ." I felt despair over what had happened. "I did more harm than good with my anger. How am I ever going to show the children love again? How am I ever going to teach them again?"

Miss Alice sat in the overstuffed chair and listened while David poked at the fire. "Don't look so woebegone," Miss Alice smiled at me. "So thee fell into a temper. Thee is human."

Hope trickled back into my heart.

"But, Miss Alice, what about the schoolroom and the books? Someone deliberately ruined them."

"That's right," David spoke up. "We can't let that pass."

"No, we can't," Miss Alice agreed, "and we shan't."

9

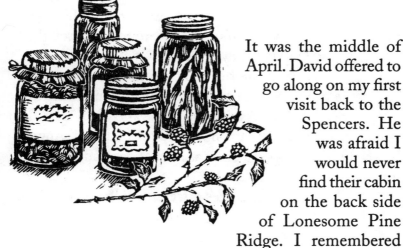

It was the middle of April. David offered to go along on my first visit back to the Spencers. He was afraid I would never find their cabin on the back side of Lonesome Pine Ridge. I remembered my first experience back in January and knew he was probably right.

A warm touch of spring caressed the air as we walked along. The evergreens were tipped with bright green now, and the willows overhanging the streams were a whisper of green lace. Here and there in the fields of the valley, spicewood bushes waved yellow plumes. David and I laughed as we walked. It was spring, and I felt light and carefree, glad to leave my troubles at school behind.

As we reached the top of the ridge, I hardly recognized the Spencer place. Gone were the ice and snow and that eerie feeling I had experienced when the mailman, Ben Pentland, first brought me here. All around us were the rich odors of sunbaked earth and pine and spruce and balsam. Entering the cabin was like sticking one's nose into one of those souvenir pillows filled with cedar chips they made for the tourists back home in Asheville.

Fairlight Spencer had arranged leaves around some violets in two old pewter bowls. "The very first," she told us as she fondled the flowers. Even though this Tennessee mountain woman's hands were red and rough, I noticed how ladylike they were.

Fairlight showed me her quilt stretched in the quilting frame near the hearth. "Mama aims to make me one after a spell." It was Clara's voice. She and Zady had just come into the room carrying heaping plates of gingerbread. David grabbed a piece as it went past, and the girls giggled.

"Say! This is good. Tastes different. What's in it?" he asked.

"Made out of sorghum and wheaten flour," Zady explained.

Next John brought in a cedar pail filled with roasted chestnuts. Then Fairlight's husband, Jeb, appeared with an antique instrument under his arm. "Howdy do, ma'am. Howdy, Preacher." He almost sang his words. "How's the steeple making at the church?"

"Coming along, Jeb. Much too slow to suit me though. I've got to knock off for a while now to string telephone wire. Christy wrote letters back home and got folks to donate wire to us. Say, Jeb, how about giving me a hand with the wire stringing?"

"Aye. Been thinkin' I might lend you a hand with something. Truth is, I'd kinder like to speak into that newfangled contraption myself."

Jeb pulled out the instrument and began plying the goose quill back and forth across the strings. It was one of those old-time dulcimers. With a slender waist and heart-shaped holes, the shape of the instrument was different than a guitar. It had four strings, and its tone had a clear, flutelike quality as Jeb played and sang.

> Oh, as I went down to Derby Town
> All on a summer's day,
> It's there I saw the finest ram
> That was ever fed on hay . . .
>
> Oh, the wool upon this ram's back
> It drug to the ground,
> And I hauled it to the market
> And it weighed ten thousand pounds . . .

The girls squealed with delight. Jeb told a story that went on for sixteen verses. It ushered me into the land of castles and snow white steeds and the moors of England and Scotland.

As the concert ended, Mrs. Spencer sought me out. "Miz Christy, could I speak with you?" She pulled me away from the others to the far corner of the room.

"You've got a heap of young'uns in the school for one gal-woman," she gently said. "Is there anything I can do to holp, like clean up the school? I'm a good hand to work. Or wash some of your go-to-meetin' clothes? It's my turn to favor you now."

"Mrs. Spencer, that's the nicest offer anyone has made me since I left home. You're right. Sixty-seven children are a handful and I do need help." I groped for the right words. "I'll accept your wonderful offer. Maybe there'll be something I can do for you, too."

Her face broke into a wide smile. "Aye, you can holp, Miz Christy." Suddenly her voice sank to a whisper. "I cain't read nor write. Would you learn me how?"

"I'd love to, Mrs. Spencer. Could you come down to the mission house, maybe Saturday?"

"For shore and certain, I'll be there," she answered joyously. "Oh, and would you handle my front name? It's Fairlight."

As David and I walked back to the mission a short while later, I felt lighthearted. I spotted a pink flower and skipped over to pluck it. Its gentle smell brushed the air, and I waved it under David's nose.

"Isn't life wonderful!" I exclaimed with joy.

David smiled at my exuberance. "I like you when you're like this, Christy. You're full of fire."

"Oh, David, there are so many things I want to do something about."

"I'm sure you will, Christy."

David placed his hand on my arm for a brief moment then let it slide off. I felt secure walking beside him.

I don't know what the record is for learning to read, but the prize probably belongs to Fairlight Spencer. In the first lesson, she learned the alphabet and some simple words such as man, trees, light, sun, and sky. By the end of the second session, she could recognize many words and read short sentences. Three long sessions were all she needed.

After Fairlight's formal reading lessons ended, she and I still saw each other every week. I soon discovered all sorts of hidden mountain treasures through my new friend.

One day, I found a bunch of wildflowers on my desk. Another time she left me a basket filled with berries. Other surprises lurked around each corner. She began to bring me jars of wild blackberry jelly or a poem she had copied. One time she left me a tiny basket lined with moss and three robins' eggshells. It was her way of sharing the beauty of the eggs' blue color.

Fairlight Spencer knew how to enjoy life, and this amazed me. Here was a woman who had a husband and five children. She had to sew their clothes, cook, clean, and wash. And she didn't even have electricity or piped-in water. Yet she never felt sorry for herself.

"It's today I must be livin'," she would tell me. And live she did. There was always time for a story in front of the fire with the children snuggled against her. Frequently, she would stop her work and call the children to enjoy the first spring blossoms or gaze at the twinkling night sky.

As spring budded, the two of us often romped through the woods like a pair of female pied pipers. The children would race ahead of us swinging on the limbs of trees or wading in the creeks. Squeals of glee would echo through the forest as we laughed and played.

One afternoon, Fairlight and I set out on our own to explore.

"Fairlight," I said as we dried our wet toes in a bed of ferns, "let's climb to that knob up Lonesome Pine Ridge today."

"Miz Christy, that knob is a fer piece, more'n four good looks and a right smart walk." She winked at me. "But we'll give it a try."

The two of us struck out through the scrub woods toward the base of the mountain. The trail slowly wound upwards. This surprised me because I thought we would go straight up the face of the mountain. That showed how much I knew. We still had several thousand feet to climb!

Soon we were reaching for a laurel bush or a rhododendron to hang on to. Blackberry bushes and thorns slashed at our faces as we stumbled over roots in the path.

"Time to lay off and rest yourself," Fairlight directed at last. With aching calves, I sank on a nearby rock. Much of the mountain still towered above us.

Before long, we were off again, plunging through the belt of hardwood trees, sugar maples, beeches, and yellow birches. From there we pushed into a fragrant grove of balsam and red cedar. It was a fairy-like place of drifting clouds and shafts of light, with a clean carpet of ferns and mosses everywhere. At any moment I expected to see a group of elves pop out from behind one of the trees. The two of us traipsed on.

It was late in the afternoon when we finally reached the top. The entire world lay at our feet. Fairlight sat behind me, silently hugging her knees. I had learned by now that stillness was a part of these mountain people. Their quiet mirrored the silence of the nature that surrounded them. And their friendships ran as deep as the valleys we had trooped through. Fairlight would be my friend for life, and I would be hers. That was the mountain way.

Lying flat on my stomach, I inched close to the edge of the rock shelf. My eyes drank in the thundering waves of greens and smoky blues spread out below. The majesty of the scene captured my heart and soul. Here I was looking at natural beauty.

Yet life was not always beautiful like this. These mountains were full of poverty and ignorance. And I was learning how deeply hatred had seeped into these people's lives.

As I lay there, I thought about Little Burl and Mountie, and my heart warmed. Where else could I look over a summit at such magnificence? Where else could I meet a Fairlight or a Little Burl or a Miss Alice? Only here in these mountains. I remembered David touching my arm, and I longed to know him better. And Miss Alice. I could learn so much from her. She understood why she was living and where she belonged.

The question Miss Alice asked me rose up in my thoughts. *Was I supposed to stay here?* I asked myself. *Was there a purpose behind it?* As I stared at the horizon, I began to sense the answer. *Look deeper into the lives of these people, Christy. Treasures wait for you behind the wall of their poverty. Open your heart. You will see.*

I glanced around at Fairlight who smiled back at me. Yes, somewhere through her and the others, I would find what I was looking for. I would understand why I had to come.

10

When Lundy Taylor didn't return to school for more than a week after I'd yanked his hair, I decided to pay a call on his father, Bird's Eye Taylor. Saddling up Theo, I started off one afternoon.

The Taylor cabin had been built between two rock planes forming the top of a small mountain. It was the most isolated place I had ever seen, more like a fortress than a home. The final ascent was so steep that I tied Theo to a tree two hundred feet below the cabin and climbed the rest of the way on foot.

"Hello-o-o!" I yelled through cupped hands. "Mr. Taylor, I want to talk to you. May I come up?"

The figure of a grizzly man stood in the empty doorway. He was dressed in a shabby plaid shirt and baggy trousers. His black felt hat had holes in it, and the brim was turned down all around. He was holding a shotgun in his right hand. I realized he'd been watching me all the way up the mountain.

"Come up then," he replied grudgingly.

I climbed the hard-packed, slippery path. "Mr. Taylor, I'm Christy Huddleston, the new teacher," I panted.

"What d'you want with us?" The man's glaring face had not been shaved in days.

"We've been missing Lundy at school. I wondered why he hasn't been there."

"You know why," he said coldly.

"May I come in?"

Surprised by my question, the man moved to one side. For the first time I saw Lundy crouching behind his father.

The inside of the cabin felt like a cave. Only a stone chimney, two straight chairs, and a warped table furnished the room. A heavy coating of dust and soot covered everything. With one foot, Mr. Taylor shoved one of the chairs across the floor in my direction. He threw his legs across the seat of another one and plopped down.

"We don't confidence women teachers none," he said hatefully, rubbing his hand over his stubbled chin. "Want to whop my young'uns my own self. Don't want no gal-woman a'doin' it."

"Mr. Taylor, I didn't whip Lundy."

"Didn't hide him?"

"No. Lundy is bigger than I am. Do you think I could whip him?"

At this point Lundy was already sidling toward the door. His father's hand shot out to whack at him, but the boy ducked. "Consarned fool. You lied t'me."

"Ah, Pap, I jest—"

"I'm a'going to catch hold of you and smoke your britches till the fire catches."

Lundy was out the door like a jackrabbit.

"Don't be too hard on him, Mr. Taylor. Lundy was testing me out, that's all. I had some trouble with him. I had to talk sternly to him. And I *did* jerk him by the hair."

For the first time, there was something close to a thaw on Bird's Eye's face. He didn't seem to think yanking Lundy's hair such a bad idea.

"I hope you'll send him back," I said as I rose to leave. "I want him to return."

I hurried down the slope as fast as I could. I had the feeling Lundy was spying on me from behind a bush somewhere, but I didn't wait to find out.

The boy returned a week later. On that Friday, I was working at my desk during the noon recess. The children were playing hide-and-go-seek outside. Suddenly, I heard shouts and angry voices. I dropped my pen and rushed to see what was happening. The children were out of sight around the corner.

"I'll crunch you, you little—"

"Dirty bully!"

"Shut your mouth, I'll knock your block—"

"Oh, shinny on your tintype!"

"Weasel!"

A tight circle of children hid the identity of the fighters.

"Hit's Teacher! Better stop it!"

The children made a path for me. I saw Festus Allen, Little Burl's older brother, and Lundy Taylor fighting.

Eleven-year-old Festus was flailing his fists and kicking his feet. Blood streamed from his nose.

"Quit that this instant!" I wedged myself between the two boys and only barely missed getting a fist in my face. Festus was shaking mad. "No Taylor's gonna lay out my brother and git by with it."

Then I saw Little Burl, white and limp, stretched out on the ground. I bent over him. He was unconscious!

"Someone run quick! Dip a rag in cold water and bring it to me." My hands felt the little boy's heart. Beating, thank God! But there was a round, red mark on his stomach.

Ruby Mae thrust a wet cloth into my hand. I cradled the six-year-old boy in my arms and gently dabbed the cloth on his forehead. "Little Burl, it's Teacher. Can you hear me?"

It seemed forever before the youngster's eyelids fluttered open. "Hurts, Teacher," he moaned. "My stomach hurts."

"Just lie still. I'll hold you."

As I sat on the ground, I looked up at the circle of faces. Lundy wasn't there.

"How'd this happen?" I asked them.

Ruby Mae spoke up. "I was standin' behind one of them gopher trees thar, Teacher," she explained. "Little Burl was a-scroungin' around under the schoolhouse. Lundy seed him and shrieked like a panther. Then he took out after Burl. Started kickin' him."

"Ruby Mae, would you go to the house and ask Mr. Grantland to come here? Tell him I need him."

I helped Little Burl to his feet, and the children and I walked with him slowly to the schoolhouse steps. Lundy Taylor sat inside by himself in a corner of the classroom.

"Lundy, get in your seat and stay there. I'll be back in a minute," I ordered from outside the door as the children went back in.

Ruby Mae and David were coming up the hill. I sent Ruby Mae inside, and turned toward David. "Why would Lundy kick Little Burl for looking under the floor?"

"I can't answer that one, Christy. Lundy's big and sometimes brutal, but even he would need a powerful reason to kick a little boy unconscious. Let me handle this one."

I was relieved. "That's fine with me, David."

David left, and I walked up the steps to the schoolroom. Lundy was gone.

11

All afternoon
I waited for
some report
from David,
but none
came. Finally,
toward dusk I decided to
investigate myself. I crossed the plank sidewalk from the
mission house to the school. As I stood at the front steps,
something gave me an uneasy feeling. What was it? I tried
the door. It was locked. Everything seemed in order. Then
I realized what was wrong. The pigs under the building
weren't making their usual scratching and rooting noises.
And what was that horrible smell? I picked up my skirts
and ran back to the big house.

"What's the hurry, Christy?" David had just returned
and met me on the porch.

"Something's wrong—at the schoolhouse. Will you
have a look?"

I trailed his long strides across the yard and up the hill. That same strong odor drifted through the evening breeze. As David and I turned the corner at the back of the building, I stumbled over a broken jug. Several hogs were stretched out asleep, breathing heavily.

David stopped and stared. He walked around the sleeping pigs and even poked a few with his foot. They snored on. Then he stooped to look under the floor. "I'm going to have a look, Christy."

I could hear him moving some boards under the building. Then he whistled loudly. "Holy thunder!"

"What, David?"

"Somebody's fixed a place under the floor like a little storage room. It's full of jugs. Moonshine whiskey. Here, I'll hand them to you one at a time."

I set the heavy jugs on the ground, one after another. Finally David came out, rubbing dust off his hands. "So this was what Lundy didn't want Burl to find! But, Christy, the storage room is too well planned. No boy could've done that carpentry work." David paused for breath. "Christy, I think someone is making illegal whiskey back here in the mountains and channeling it under the schoolhouse building to sell it on the outside."

"But why this building?"

"A brilliant move, like hiding something in the most obvious place so it's missed. The pieces are beginning to fit. You remember Uncle Bogg warning me about the strangers? Well, I'm afraid we've got a little moonshining business going on right under our noses. And I think some of our schoolboys make the deliveries."

I was speechless. I stood looking at David, trying to grasp it. "David, do you really think some of our boys are involved? Isn't that dangerous?"

"Yes. We need to talk with Miss Alice as soon as possible. I'm going to find out who's using these boys. And I need to find the still."

Suddenly I was afraid for David. As if sensing this, he reached for my hand. "Do you have to go after the moonshiners yourself, David? You know as well as I do these men won't stand meddlers."

"I know. But I can't get the federal marshals on the case without more evidence. These mountain men can guzzle all the corn liquor they please, but when they start involving our schoolchildren—"

We both gazed at the odd scene in front of us. "David, those pigs still haven't moved. Do you suppose . . . ? No, it couldn't be."

"Yes, it could!" David's eyes glared like a reflecting windowpane. "Remember my telling you that horses like Prince won't drink a drop of water with mash in it? Well, pigs like nothing better. These hogs are drunk!"

"How funny," I chuckled.

David managed a slight smile. "The pigs may be funny," he said, "but what's happening here isn't!"

Every Tuesday evening, Miss Alice met with David and me in her cabin. These regular weekly conferences helped us discuss the week gone by and plan for the week ahead. Miss Alice made these evenings a refreshing oasis in the midst of our busy lives.

On this particular Tuesday night, David sank gratefully into her red wing chair. He stretched his long legs and sniffed the brewing coffee. Both Miss Alice and I knew he had important news to discuss.

"I found the still," he said abruptly.

Miss Alice's hand, pouring a cup of coffee, paused in midair. "What still? Whose is it?"

"I don't know. The moonshiners weren't there. The still had just been moved."

Miss Alice finished pouring the coffee as we listened intently to David.

"Yesterday afternoon, Prince and I started in the direction of Big Lick Gap. You know how good the water at Coldsprings Branch is. Well, after we got to the Branch, Prince stopped and stretched his long neck down to drink. Then he began acting strangely—sniffed the water, snorted, and backed away. Wouldn't drink a drop.

"Right away, I knew something was wrong. I got off and cupped up some water in my hands. You couldn't miss the smell of mash. I knew a still had to be upstream so I started to follow the stream to its source. When I found some broken branches and a piece of copper tubing lying in the leaves, I decided not to go on.

"I didn't dare use the new telephone here at the mission, so I rode to the telephone exchange in Lyleton and phoned the federal office in Knoxville."

David paused, sipped his coffee, then went on. "The marshals got to El Pano a little past midnight. Under last night's bright moon, they pushed on to Coldsprings Branch. What they found was a dummy stuffed with straw, swinging in the breeze like a man strung up—the usual warning message for revenue men. Somebody had warned the moonshiners, and they had cleared out just in time."

"Who could have warned them?" I voiced the question we were all thinking.

"I've no idea, but we're going to find out."

12

One Saturday in early May, David and I headed to the Holt cabin for a "Working." This was a mountain custom that dated back to pioneer times. When a barn was being raised or a house built, everyone gathered together to help. The women provided the food while the men swung axes. In many ways it felt like a holiday.

I had not visited Zacharias and little Vella's parents yet. Ozias Holt, their father, had appeared at the mission house one afternoon to invite us to help him clear Deer Mountain back of his place. By the time we arrived, some of the men were already grubbing out the tangle of huckleberry bushes, poison hemlocks, and small pines on the slope. Several looked up, but no one spoke. I noticed Bob Allen hacking some scrub oaks and once again felt thankful for the doctor's operation that first day in Cutter Gap.

Tom McHone was pulling up some rhododendrons on a stretch next to Jeb Spencer and Bird's Eye Taylor. Jeb smiled when he saw us, but Bird's Eye scowled at us from his work spot on the hill.

"Howdy, Miz Christy. Mornin', Preacher." Mr. Holt met us in patched overalls and the familiar dirty, torn, felt hat. His grey beard was short around his chin but bushy at the sides of his face. With a gnarled forefinger, he pointed to the strip he had saved for David.

I wanted to stay in the open air and watch the men, but Fairlight motioned me inside. By now, I was getting used to such smells as corn pone and bacon grease, wood smoke and snuff. But I was still having trouble with the animal smells. The room was already crowded. Opal McHone was helping Ozias's wife, Rebecca, set up a table of pine boards for the noon meal. Fairlight and Clara were pushing back five straw mattresses against the wall to make room. The Holts had eight children altogether, and I spied four dirty faces with running noses peering down at me from the top of the ladder leading to the loft.

Ordinarily, a Working was a happy time. Women would keep their hands busy with quilt pieces or stringing shucky green beans. Some of the men would bring fiddles or dulcimers.

But today something was different. Fairlight's clouded face alerted me to trouble ahead. The women were unusually quiet, like the silence before a huge storm. I couldn't escape the feeling that a black cloud hovered overhead.

At noon, the men walked in for the midday meal. It was the mountain custom for the men to eat first and for the women to serve them. The women ate afterward.

"Preacher-parson, will you wait prayer on the table for us?" Ozias Holt asked.

David stood up. In a deep voice he prayed, "For the bounty of this table, for the hands that prepared this food, for this home, for friends to help us, Lord, we give Thee our thanks. Amen."

He looked beaten. His broad shoulders sagged, and his cotton shirt dripped with sweat. As he reached for a piece of cornbread, I saw the insides of his hands. They looked like raw meat.

"Just listen to them women cacklin' like hens," Uncle Bogg tried to liven things up. "Just t'other day I asked a woman-person to show me her tongue. Wanted to see if it was wore down. She couldn't stop cacklin' long enough even to show it to me."

Mrs. Holt lashed back as if on cue. "Confound it, you ugly old coot. Got no time to fool with you. I'll feather into you and sweep you out of here like you was dust."

Laughter rippled across the room. The toothless Uncle Bogg now had his audience in hand.

"Uncle Bogg," Ozias Holt said. "I've got it in mind that you might tell us that tale about the preacher named Dry Guy."

Something inside me turned icy. *Why this story today?* I wondered. Dry Guy was a familiar story about a preacher who had once come to the mountains. The mountaineers didn't like him and he ended up dead. I had already heard the story and didn't want to hear it again, but Uncle Bogg didn't have to be asked twice. He told the story with all its gruesome details.

Later that afternoon, I left the quilt-piecing to peek outside. Several of the men had already finished their strips. David still had almost half to clear. I knew he wouldn't accept any help, but I wished someone would offer. He knew these mountain men would listen to his preaching on Sunday only if he could prove himself as a man here on a regular work day.

When I brought David a dipper of cool water, he drank every drop. I winced at his bloody right hand. "David, let me bandage it," I pleaded.

"No." He shook his head grimly. "I'd better finish this way. You can doctor me this evening."

I went back inside. About an hour later, we heard shouting. Fairlight and I rushed to the front door.

"Ain't been treated so fine today, have ye, Preacher?" Bird's Eye's taunting voice was slurred and thick. At once, I knew he'd been drinking moonshine. "Here's what we think of folks that pester with other folks' business." He spat on the ground. "You'uns and your religion." He spat again. "You keep your religion inside the cupboard in the church house where it belongs, or I'll give you this—" Bird's Eye raised his rifle.

I clapped my hands over my mouth to stifle a scream. Three rapid shots spattered into the ground at David's feet. The fourth whistled within inches of his head. David did not flinch.

My heart beat wildly. No one moved. David did not speak. Slowly his deep brown eyes traveled across the circle of men. He did nothing. Finally Bird's Eye lowered his rifle and began shuffling his feet in the dust. The air was so quiet that a cow mooing on a distant mountain-side sounded like a bugle call.

At last David spoke, "If any of you would like to hear my answer to this, come to church tomorrow."

Then he picked up his axe and attacked the last of the bushes on his strip.

By Sunday morning, every person in Cutter Gap had heard about Bird's Eye and the Working. The little schoolhouse was packed. Everyone was there. Jeb and Fairlight Spencer sat in the right front row with their five children. The O'Teales occupied the other side. I noticed a barefoot Mountie holding the coat with the big buttons in her lap even though it was May. Tom McHone had gotten Opal to come today. He balanced Little Toot on one knee while Isaak held young Vincent. I didn't see the Allens but knew they'd come soon.

A mass of other wriggling children and rustling Sunday school papers crammed the room, too. A couple of mangy hound dogs circled around the bucket of fresh drinking water. Only David, Miss Ida, and I had dressed for the service. Everybody else wore their regular work clothes. The men who filtered in spit brown streams of tobacco juice just outside the church door. I sat near the back nervously picking at my nails.

David looked tired today but handsome. His pinstriped pants, white shirt, and black tie made him look like he could have stepped into the pulpit of any city church, yet here we were in the backwoods of the Smoky Mountains. I was proud of him for yesterday.

He stepped up to the wooden podium and the room grew still. "Certain things have happened in the Cove these last few days that have made me change my sermon," he began.

Some of the people leaned forward. The men still in the yard crowded up to the doors and windows to listen.

"There are those among us who think Christianity is just for Sundays. Some of you feel a preacher should quit after his sermon and shut his eyes to everything going on outside the church. Some of you have even told me to mind my own business."

David leaned forward. "Friends, the church's business is my business. The church is not just a building; it's a fellowship of people who want Christ to be their leader. But where does He lead? What does He say?" David's eyes swept his listening congregation. "Jesus would tell us that 'no man can serve two masters.' You can't serve Christ on Sunday, and then serve evil on Monday night."

I was caught up by what David was saying. His words were powerful.

"Men and women, in this Cove there are those who are working at night and serving evil."

I felt my throat go dry. I dared not look at anyone. Prickles ran up and down my spine. David was going to do it. He was going to look evil straight in the eye.

"The white lightning that's being brewed here is the devil's own brew. You and I both know it leads to fights and killings. And now, some of our schoolboys are being used to help sell this liquor."

David's voice grew stronger. "Folks, the Christian religion is not a thing. It's not like a piece of paper we can squirrel away in the cubbyhole of a rolltop desk. Christ Himself declared war against the sin and evil in our world. Wrongs must be brought into the light of day. And believe me that includes the evil right here in our own Cutter Gap."

As David was preaching, I felt a tap on the shoulder. Startled, I jumped. When I turned around, Dr. MacNeill whispered, "Can you come with me? It's an emergency. Little Burl."

Little Burl! I quickly followed the doctor out the back door and down the plank steps.

"Miss Huddleston, I'm going to have to operate. Will you help? I wouldn't ask you, but there's no one else. Alice Henderson is at Big Lick."

I didn't know if I could do it. Just the smell of ether made me sick. But this was Little Burl.

I walked with the doctor quickly down the hill toward the mission house. "What's wrong with him?" I asked.

"He has a torn muscle in his stomach, and it's gotten infected. I've got to drain the infection or he'll die."

Doubts about my ability to handle this lay like a sleeping cat on the back porch of my mind. I couldn't get Bob Allen's operation out of my mind. However, a few minutes later I had mounted Prince and was riding beside the doctor out of the mission yard. Our destination was Blackberry Creek, two miles away.

"Did something happen to Little Burl at school? Was he in a fight?" The doctor rode ahead of me and yelled back.

"Not exactly. Last week, he discovered something hidden under the schoolhouse. Lundy Taylor tackled him and kicked him in the stomach. Festus and Lundy got into a fight over it. Little Burl had a red mark on his stomach that turned black and blue, but I didn't think it was serious."

We rode on in silence. Panic seeped up in me like bubbles in hot chocolate. *How could this have happened? Will I do the right thing? Miss Alice should be here. I'm not the one to do this.*

The rhododendron were beginning to bloom. Their fluffy pink blossoms trailed down the hillside. It was May in the mountains, beautiful and colorful. But I couldn't enjoy the scenery. I was too absorbed by my own fear. Then, a series of thoughts swirled up from some deep cavern within. Only these were not thoughts of panic; they were orderly and clear. *Miss Alice isn't the one for this job. You are. Get your attention off the problem and look at Me. I am greater than any problem. You are about to discover this for yourself.*

Had I prayed? No, not consciously. How odd that I now no longer felt alone. Gratitude swelled inside me. I found myself saying "Thank You" over and over. Somehow, the problem was gone. My heart soared like a hawk. It was a miracle. And I was on the way to help precious Little Burl.

13

Once we reached the Allens, everything happened quickly. Little Burl's blue eyes showed joy when he saw that Teacher had come to be with him. "You'll stay right with me? Hit won't hurt?"

"Of course not. I'll hold your hand." The youngster looked so tiny in that big bed with Scalawag, the raccoon, curled up beside him. Creed had let his little brother borrow the animal for the operation.

Mary Allen, Little Burl's mother, looked more upset this time than she had been at the time of her husband's head operation at the Spencers. "Something's awful wrong," she moaned over and over in her rocking chair, "awful wrong in Burl's belly."

When I sniffed the sickly sweet smell of ether, I sat down by the six-year-old boy. Rob and Creed and the other three Allen children huddled in a far corner.

"I'm going to tell you a story now, Burl. It's about the wicked Hoptoad and little Yellow Dragon. Now this was a beautiful dragon, and he lived right down by the edge of your own Blackberry Creek. . . ."

Light from the kerosene lantern flickered shadows across the boy's small, white face. For a moment the only sound was the boiling and bubbling of the water in the washpot on the open fire. But then Mrs. Allen began wailing. "He won't never wake up. I knowed he won't never wake up." The doctor ordered Bob, her husband, to take her out of the room.

Even though this particular Sunday was bright and sunny, the Allen's rustic cabin was dark and dreary. To get more light, Dr. MacNeill asked Creed to open the cabin door. But then the chickens wandered in. One rooster strutted over to the bed and began flapping his wings, getting ready to hop up. We chose fourteen-year-old Rob to shoo the chickens and rooster away and guard the entrance.

Bob Allen stood with his son at the door and waited. The other children didn't say a word. At each step of the operation, I found myself hanging on to that strong Presence I had experienced on the ride over. The ether didn't bother me, and I was able to follow the doctor's instructions.

"There," Dr. MacNeill said gently as he finished, "he'll be all right now. Bob, you and Mary stay with Burl. Miss Huddleston, let's take a break."

I wiped my hands on the apron I was wearing and heaved a sigh of relief. The doctor had removed all of the infection in Little Burl's stomach muscle. With rest and care, he would be fine.

The doctor led the way along the path to Bob Allen's water-powered mill, down at the creek among the willows. Water from the spring rains raced down the flume onto a water wheel almost as tall as the one-room mill. The doctor opened the creaking door to the building and stood aside for me to enter. Inside, the last rays of sun filtered through the corn dust hanging in the air.

"Was it blockade whiskey Little Burl found?" His question was abrupt.

I nodded. "Little Burl found the hiding place."

"I thought so." He leaned against the grain sacks piled beside the wall. "I heard just enough of the sermon. David's declared war on moonshining."

"Of course . . ."

The doctor held up his hand. "Let me talk first," he interrupted. "There's more you and David need to know. I was the one who warned the moonshiners that David was on his way to the federal marshals."

My lips formed the question, "You?"—but no sound came.

"I had good reason for informing, Miss Huddleston. I had to choose the lesser of two evils. What I mean is that I had to choose between letting this still go a little longer or more feuding and killing."

"What do you mean?"

"Someone spied Bob Allen coming out of David's bunkhouse the other night."

I hesitated before responding. "Bob did visit David but he only offered to help David find the still. He didn't know where it was either."

"It doesn't matter. The person who saw Bob told the men making the moonshine, and they *thought* he tipped

David off. If David or the marshals had found the still, and Bird's Eye had been taken by the law . . ."

"So Bird's Eye is one of the culprits?"

"Sure. And even if David got Bird's Eye Taylor behind bars, there'd be plenty of others left on the Taylor side of this fight. No matter what Bob did, he'd still be the number-one target. You see, it's the Taylors and the Allens who've had the feud all along."

The doctor wiped his finger across the dusty windowpanes. "There's something else. Tom McHone is part of it."

"Opal McHone's husband? Uncle Bogg's son? Does Opal know?" My thoughts raced with questions.

"I don't know. Up to now Tom has always stayed away from stilling."

"Then why now?"

"Because Opal's been sick since she lost her baby girl this past winter. She has needed medicine and food, and these things cost money. Tom would let me supply the medicine, but he's too proud to take food."

The doctor paused. "Back in these mountains there's only one real source of money and that's the sale of good whiskey to outlanders. Tom's a good man, Miss Huddleston. I just couldn't see a man like him turned in."

At that moment, the mill door flew open. It was Rob. "Burl's waking up. Papa said for you to come, Doc."

I shoved my questions to the back of my mind as we hurried back up the path to check on Little Burl. But I realized I had to find some answers to all of this somewhere, and soon.

14

"Teacher! Teacher! There's a ruckus in the yard tonight. Prince is a-carryin' on something fearful."

"What do you mean, Ruby Mae?" I asked as I scooted back my chair from the dining room table.

"He's a-bangin' the sides of his stall, a-snortin' and a-pawin'."

I put down the papers I was grading and rushed with Ruby Mae to the stable. Even in the dark, we could see the door was open. *David is always so careful to close and latch it,* I thought.

The familiar odors of hay and manure and leather met us as the door creaked on its metal hinges. Prince was pawing and kicking the sides of his stall. The light of my kerosene lantern first fell across David's saddle. The saddle was lying on the floor and had been slashed over and over, its insides ripped out and flung on the floor beside it. Alarmed, I ran forward to look at Prince. I nearly dropped the lamp when I saw him.

"Mercy me!" Ruby Mae shrieked.

The stallion's long black mane, tail, and forelocks had been sheared off and were lying in the hay at his feet. I thrust the lamp into Ruby Mae's hands and examined his flanks, searching for cuts or wounds. Thankfully, I found none.

Prince! Our beautiful black stallion with the white star on his head. My answer to prayer. The horse looked pathetic and he knew it. He nuzzled me with his soft moist nose, then put his head on my shoulder. A pool of tears stood in my eyes.

"Hit's the meanest job I ever seed. Now who would do a thing like that?"

"I wish I knew, Ruby Mae. Go tell Mr. Grantland. Only I'm not sure I can bear to look at his face when he sees this. I'll stay with Prince."

Ruby Mae had not gotten far when I heard her scream, "Holp! Holp! Teacher—Mr. Grantland—Quick! Somebody, come quick!"

I dashed to the barn door. A mass of flames shot up from something in front of the schoolhouse. I picked up my skirts and ran toward the fire. David had heard the screams from his bunkhouse. We reached the spot together and instantly recognized the wooden pulpit from the church. It had been carried into the yard and set on fire.

"We've got to keep embers from leaping to the church roof," David ordered. "Buckets! We need buckets and everybody's help."

Ruby Mae and David bolted for the house, calling Miss Ida. Soon we had a bucket brigade going. After the fifth pail of water, the fire began to sizzle and die. The four of us stood in the moonlight staring at the charred pulpit.

"David, this isn't all." I swallowed hard. "There's more. It's Prince."

"He's not—not dead?"

"No, thank God. Not that. But it's bad. His hair, it's all been cut off. It's awful!"

The next day David told the schoolchildren. Poor Prince was on display in the stable yard most of the day. The children stood in clusters staring at the horse and growing more angry by the hour.

"He was so purty with that long mane a-sweeping back in the wind," Creed sighed as he chewed on a piece of straw.

"And with his tail a-flying . . ." Zacharias Holt added shaking his head.

"Now he looks plumb unnatural, like a mule." Isaak McHone kept walking round and round the horse in disbelief.

"Oh, Isaak, pet him. He can't holp it." Clara Spencer got up from the log she was sitting on and walked toward the animal.

"No, but not holping it don't mend it," Isaak answered back.

Nine-year-old Sam Houston scratched his blond head and bit his bottom lip. "Look at them flies a-pesterin' him. Now Prince don't have nothing to kick 'em off with."

"Reckon we could take turns a-fanning the flies off him?" Zacharias brightened at the idea of helping.

"Wish I could knock-fight the living daylights out of them that done it." Creed balled both hands into a fist and narrowed his eyes.

The next day, David appeared in school to make an announcement. "Children, there are some folks in Cutter Gap who hate the church and me and even Prince. They want to run us out and close down the church and the school. Well, that would be wrong."

The children listened intently. The youngsters in the Cove had always been fond of David. They were on his side, and they wanted to do battle for him and his horse.

"We don't scare that easily. We're going to fight back, but not with fists or guns. I have a plan."

Instantly, the children began wiggling in their seats. This might be good! David continued.

"I've saved the hair from Prince's mane and tail. If you'll help me make this hair into watch fobs, we'll sell them and buy a new saddle and a new pulpit. What do you say?"

Hands flew up across the room. David set up sawhorse tables in the stable yard. Every evening after school, the boys and girls twirled strands of horse hair into chains for pocket watches. David made a long list of people and organizations, and I agreed to help him write the letters. In each letter we told the story, enclosed a watch fob, and asked for a donation in return.

The response was overwhelming. Over $350 flowed in. It was enough to replace the pulpit and Prince's saddle, buy new hymnbooks, and even purchase a second horse named Buttons.

And Prince? He became the most petted and beloved animal in the Cove.

15

One morning toward the end of May, I stood on the back porch shaking the crumbs out of the tablecloth for Miss Ida. We had just finished breakfast. As I looked out, I spotted someone riding a horse toward the mission yard. A second rider behind him was pointing a Winchester rifle at the one in front. Another man wearing a grey hat and matching grey clothes marched beside a horse with something doubled over in the saddle. Instantly, I realized it was a man's body.

As they got closer, I recognized Bird's Eye Taylor with his hands cuffed and chained to his saddlebow. *There must have been a successful raid*, I thought. *But where's Tom? Oh, no!* My heart sank into my stomach.

"Miss, I'm Gentry Long, United States Marshal." The second rider's voice carried clearly across the yard. "We've got a wounded man here. Can you help?"

Already I was running toward the yard.

"We didn't want to take this man clear to Lyleton," he explained as he dismounted. "He's lost too much blood. Can you get a doctor? We need to carry this prisoner on to the jail."

"Of course." I had been right. The wounded one was Tom McHone. His face was white and his shirt blood-stained. He was unconscious.

David appeared and immediately took charge, helping one of the marshals carry Tom into the house. My job was to get school underway as quickly as possible. The children would be arriving any minute, and they were going to ask questions. I rushed upstairs to get my school-books.

On the way down, I paused. "How bad is it, David?"

"Tom's lost a lot of blood. We've sent for Dr. MacNeill and for Opal."

"What happened?"

"Don't know yet." David's eyes focused on my armload of books. "Have a good day, Christy," he told me. "For a few hours forget all this and concentrate on the children."

That afternoon after school, I passed the door of Tom's bedroom. Dr. MacNeill sat by his bed.

"How is he?" I whispered as I tiptoed in.

The doctor glanced up. "Sleeping now. I think he'll make it though. He was wounded by a thirty-two calibre Smith and Wesson Special. The bullet penetrated his left shoulder and lodged in his lower back. Miss Alice helped me remove it earlier. Is Opal still downstairs?"

"She's down with Miss Ida and Miss Alice getting a cup of coffee. Fairlight's with her, too. Opal seems to be relieved that Tom's stilling is finally out in the open."

A few days passed by. By the fourth day, however, the federal marshal had not dropped by to check on Tom. I was puzzled.

On the fifth day, I was carrying a pile of torn sheets for bandages up to Tom's room. As I started back down the stairs, I heard the doctor's voice, "How much do I know about what?"

"About the moonshining and how Tom was shot."

David and Dr. MacNeill were talking in the parlor.

"Are you accusing me?" Dr. MacNeill seemed irritated.

"Of sitting on information, yes."

"You're meddling in stuff you know nothing about, Preacher." The doctor stormed out of the parlor and slammed the front door.

Questions swirled through my head. *Why hasn't a marshal come back for Tom? What happened out there?* A picture sprang into my mind. *Wait a minute! The agent walking behind Bird's Eye held a gun, but . . .* The picture grew clearer . . . *he was holding a Winchester, not a Smith and Wesson.* The thought washed over me like water on a scrub board. *Tom wasn't shot by a federal agent at all. He must have been shot by Bird's Eye. That means that Dr. MacNeill didn't tip off the feds about the second location of the still. It must have been Tom!*

That afternoon, our new telephone rang. It was the jailer at Lyleton wanting to speak to David. Bird's Eye Taylor had escaped from the Lyleton jail.

I caught up with Dr. MacNeill in the mission yard late the next evening after he had checked on Tom.

"I need to talk to you," I said, a bit out of breath.

He looked at me in surprise, his sandy-red eyebrows raised. "Well, Miss Huddleston, a pleasant day to you—and I'm just fine, thank you."

I smiled. "Sorry. Could we talk in the schoolroom?"

I sat down at my desk while the doctor walked around the room. I took a deep breath. "Somebody tipped off the feds on the second location of the still. Was it you?"

"No."

"If you didn't, then did Tom? Bird's Eye is out of jail running around loose in these mountains. He could shoot Tom again. You and I both know he will, if Tom squealed. Doctor, if you really care about Tom and Opal, please don't hold back information that would help us protect Tom."

He met my gaze without flinching. "Christy, I cared about Opal and Tom McHone long before you met them," he replied scratching the stubble of two days' growth on his chin. "You and David are meddling in things you don't understand."

"I understand this. Keeping a still is against the law. It's wrong, and it must be stopped."

The doctor started pacing up and down in front of my desk across the creaking floor. "Ever heard of the Whiskey Rebellion?"

"Yes," I replied with irritation.

"In the old days, much like today, there were no roads in and out of these mountains. Farmers realized they couldn't get their produce to market. The most a pack horse could carry was only eight bushels of grain, corn or rye, and that didn't buy much sugar, salt, gunpowder, or calico. So the mountain men turned their grain into whiskey. Now, the same horse cr mule could carry twice as much, and the people here were able to make a profit."

The doctor went on. "In 1791, the federal government passed a tax on whiskey to help fill the treasury after the War for Independence. The farmers protested, and that's what the history books call the Whiskey Rebellion."

His words stopped. He sat down, pulled his pipe out of his shirt pocket, and tapped it on the edge of my desk. "Miss Huddleston, try and understand. The Cove people don't see anything wrong with making the homemade brew and selling it for extra cash. They figure they grew the grain and can do what they want with it. To them it's no more wrong than making wild strawberry preserves in their kitchens."

The doctor leaned back and sucked at the stem of his pipe. "Attacking these people through sermons and preaching won't change anything. David's sermon wasn't the right approach."

I pushed back my chair and stood up. "I respect your friendship with the McHones and your compassion, Doctor. But selling whiskey isn't the only way of getting food and medicine. Why didn't Tom come to us for help?"

"Too proud. These folks want to solve their problems by themselves. Alice Henderson at least understands this."

"But Miss Alice recognizes these people need another way. She believes God will help them."

"So she does, Miss Huddleston. And what do you believe?"

"Well—I agree. God can help them through us. We can hold classes to teach them how to care for their new babies. We can show them other farming techniques. We can start quilting bees and canning sessions and sell the things we make. We can—"

The doctor pushed back his chair and stood up. His tall muscular frame loomed in front of me. "I didn't ask you what you can *do*, Miss Huddleston. I asked you what you *believe*. I don't think you really know. Maybe you should ask Miss Alice."

I was so mad at him I wanted to slap his face. I whipped around on my heels and stomped out the schoolhouse door.

16

"Miz Christy. Please wake up. Miz Christy. We need you."

An unknown hand was shaking me and pulling me out of my dream. "Miz Christy. Some men are on the porch. They're a-tryin' to break in."

Ruby Mae's frantic whispers snapped me into consciousness. I sat up in bed. "Ruby Mae, how do you know someone's trying to break in?" I asked quietly.

"I heerd them foolin' outside the house. Woke me up. I'm skeered. What'll we do?"

"You're certain they're trying to get inside the house?"

"I'm shore. They've been a-tryin' doors."

"Let's wake up Tom. He's well enough to help now."

"No use. Gone. He's lit a rag for home."

I swung my feet to the floor and grabbed my robe. In the upstairs hall, Miss Ida stood like a frozen statue at the head of the stairs. She spoke softly, "Are they after Tom? Could they be those strangers we've been seeing around here?"

Here we were, three women alone. Ordinarily David slept in his bunkhouse only a few hundred feet away, and he would have heard our cries. But tonight he was in Knoxville talking with the marshals about the moonshining.

We heard steps and muffled whispering on the porch. As I peered into the lower hall, my eyes caught the glimmer of the brass doorknob being turned. I thought of how loosely all the mission house doors were hung and of the flimsy locks and catches. Almost any tool could pry off those hinges.

Suddenly a loud voice rang out, "Hey, open up. We'uns aim to git in there." The prowlers laughed and pounded on the door with what sounded like the butt of a gun.

Ruby Mae and I bounded down the stairs and began dragging a bookcase toward the front door. Soon we had added chairs and the piano bench. Then we started toward the back door. The dining room table with chairs piled on top of it would form a barrier . . . I hoped.

The three of us paused to listen again. The men had left the front porch and were now standing at the side of the house, arguing among themselves. Ruby Mae and I crept to one of the windows to listen.

"Ye're a woodscolt, and I'm a-gonna crack your bones," one yelled. "Not till hell freezes over," said another gruffly.

Miss Ida tugged at the sleeve of my robe. "We're wasting time. Let's scout to see what we can use for weapons in case they break down one of the doors or come in through a window."

We collected a sad assortment for our arsenal: two pokers, a fireplace shovel, some planks, and three cast-iron frying pans from Miss Ida's kitchen.

The men stomped around to the front porch again. "We're goin' shiffle right through the door to git our doney gal. We're cagey."

Now I really was frightened. I felt Miss Ida's hand cover mine. "Don't answer, Christy. Not a word from you. Let me try to find out who they really are."

She went to the door. "Who are you? And what do you want?" she called out in a loud, clear voice. "I'm Ida Grantland, David's sister."

"It's the old'un, poppin' her teeth," one man said.

"We just dropped by," another voice picked up. "Ah, maw, don't be nervish now. We're not liquored up."

"You are too liquored up," Miss Ida countered. "And I want you to leave right now."

"No womenfolk are goin' tell us what to do. We come for Tom McHone."

I grabbed Miss Ida's arm. "Don't tell them Tom has gone," I whispered desperately. "They'll head right for his cabin to kill him."

"If we don't tell them," she whispered back, "then they'll get mad and break in. And who knows what they have stored in their liquored minds. Bird's Eye's out there. He's capable of anything."

111

"Let's try to stall a little longer," I pleaded. "Promise you'll wait as long as you can."

"I'll try," Miss Ida agreed.

"What's goin' on in there?" came through the door.

Miss Ida tiptoed over to the pile of furniture at the door. "Miss Henderson is going to hear this racket and be up here any minute. You'd better leave before you get in trouble."

Actually, Miss Alice's bedroom was on the far side of her cabin. She wouldn't be able to hear anything.

"We'uns not scared of her."

Then came a lull. We could hear the gurgling of liquid in a jug as it passed from hand to hand. The minutes dragged on. I began to pray.

"No hardness a'tween us," a deep voice mounted up. "We don't aim to hurt you none, jest enjoy you." The men's words grew thicker all the time.

All at once, it began raining—hard, a real gully-washer. Lightning stabbed the sky. Thunder growled. Out of the northeast a strong wind sprang up, driving the rain in horizontal sheets against the windowpanes and flooding the porch.

Ruby Mae was crouching under one of the front windows. Finally she peeked out and announced, "Hallelujah, glory be, they've gone! Can't hear nothin' a-tall except the rain."

Wearily, I lit one of the lamps. The clock read four-thirty. We listened awhile longer. Then without another word, we each crept upstairs and crawled into our beds. The nightmare was over.

A few days later, I visited Miss Alice late one after-noon after school. "I have to talk to you," I told her as she opened the door of her log cabin.

Miss Alice's grey eyes looked into mine lovingly. "Go on. I'm listening."

"Miss Alice, I don't know how to apply my faith to what's happening. I was so scared the other night when those men were threatening to break in. I barely had any faith. And I don't even know how to tell someone what I believe. I'm here in Cutter Gap because something on the inside of me pointed a finger in this direction and said, 'Go!'" I pointed and waved my right index finger high in the air.

A smile tugged at the corners of her mouth. "Christy, child, whatever is on the inside of thee, it certainly has dramatic talent."

"A few days ago, Dr. MacNeill wanted to know what I believed, and I couldn't answer him."

"That's a great discovery to make." Her eyes were sparkling now.

"I don't understand."

Miss Alice picked up a pot of tea sitting on the table beside her and poured me a cup. "Many people never stop long enough to think about the basic issues of life and death, Christy. It's quite possible to go through your whole life adopting other people's ideas, never coming to your own conclusions. What has happened to you is good."

"But, Miss Alice, how do I know what to believe? Maybe one religion *is* as good as another. How can I be sure?"

Miss Alice set the teapot down on the linen doily covering her tabletop. "Someone wisely prepared to answer your question. And He left us a way to be sure. Here, I'll write it down for you."

Miss Alice walked over to a small rolltop desk in the corner. She opened a cubbyhole, retrieved a piece of notepaper, and began to write. When she had finished, she blotted the paper, folded it, and handed it to me.

"When a doctor gives you a written perscription, you have to do what it says." She handed me the folded paper. "You move on this, and God will move. I guarantee it."

I stared at her, fascinated. The piece of paper lay warm in my hand. I wanted to look at it, but Miss Alice wasn't quite finished. "Many people think religion is dull. Some religions are dull. But believe me, Christy, Christianity isn't. It's the most fascinating, delightful thing I know. You're standing on the threshold of a great adventure, Christy. Go on now, you're dying to see what I wrote. Go—and take your first step." Gaily she waved me off.

Holding the unread note in my hand, I took off for my secret retreat. About two weeks before, I had found a special place overlooking the Cove. I skirted Coldsprings Mountain and followed the thick, black-eyed Susans growing along the path. At a giant tulip poplar, I left the trail and plunged into the woods. A few hundred yards on, I parted the laurel thicket and slipped into my sanctuary—a little, woodland room. Water tumbled into a waterfall over one of the boulders beside me. It was cool and refreshing here. Before me spread a view of Pigeonroost Hollow and Cutter Gap running together to form the Cove. I could see the mountains of Lonesome Pine Ridge to the west.

But at the moment, I wasted no time on the scenery. I had waited long enough. I pulled out the note.

> If any man will do His (the Father's) will, he shall know of the doctrine, whether it be of God, or whether I speak of myself.

I read the words slowly over and over. I felt disappointed. *Is this all there is to it?* I tried to recall Miss Alice's words. "Go and take your first step," she had said. *What first step?*

I stared at the paper for a long time. *What is the Father's will for me? Wasn't I doing His will when I came here? Does this verse mean that our understanding of God follows our obedience?*

A kaleidoscope of faces danced through my mind. David—with his jet-black hair and deep brown eyes, his intense belief in what was right. Dr. MacNeill—the way he annoyed me at times. Little Burl—freckles marching across his face, always reaching out for love. Lundy—big, brutal, but somehow one of God's creatures too. Fairlight—a princess in homespun. Tom McHone—I could see his crumpled, bloodstained body slumped over in that saddle. Opal—

Opal! My swinging thoughts stopped, like the needle of a compass finally coming to rest. *Go to Opal. Talk to Opal. Opal holds the key.*

Talk to Opal about what? She holds the key to what? I asked silently. The needle pointed steadily to this thought; it didn't move again.

I rose from the rock where I had been sitting. My legs were numb. There was the troubled Cove with its poverty and its smells and its problems. The quietness of the late afternoon lay like a lavender blanket over the mountainside and valley. The sun was low in the sky. If I hurried, I could get to Opal's before dark. Yes, I would go. I had to follow the needle's direction. I had no idea what I would say or do when I got there, but I had to go.

17

I made it to Opal's before dark. As I ran toward the house, four men with rifles suddenly stepped from the woods at my right. I stopped short, my heart thumping. Bird's Eye walked toward me, his eyes like steel.

"Come to do some more pesterin' with other folks' business?" He snarled like an animal and spat on the ground.

I dared not move. "I've come to see Opal, that's all."

"Yon." The creature jerked his head in the direction of the cabin. "Go on in, but don't try no dodge with me. I'm right nervish this evenin', little careless-like with this here hog rifle."

I remembered David telling me these highlanders wouldn't hurt a woman, but I wasn't going to take any chances. I inched forward slowly. Finally I reached the rickety porch. The wooden shutters at every window had been closed. Before I could knock, the front door swung open.

"Oh, Miz Christy! I kept wishin' and hopin' . . ." Opal's voice was soft. "You holped me a'fore. I needed you again." She seized my wrists and pulled me in. "But how could you know that I wanted you?"

"I didn't know," I replied. "I'm here because, well, God told me to come." As soon as the words were out, I regretted saying them. What would Opal think?

"He did?" she asked wonderingly. "Comin' here this evening weren't your idea?"

"No, it wasn't my idea."

"But how'd He tell you?"

"By a thought that wouldn't leave, like an order on the inside. 'Go to Opal. Opal needs you—now.'"

Opal's face showed complete joy. "Then God knows about Tom and me and Bird's Eye. He cares about us."

The tired-looking woman sank into a rocker and held out her thin arms to her children. The two younger boys came scrambling. "Look-a-here!" she reasoned. "If God would tell you to come, don't you reckon He'd talk to me, too?"

"I guess."

"Then let's ask Him to tell us what to do next," Opal urged. "Will you ask Him?"

I had not prayed aloud since Sunday school, but I plunged in. "God, this is all new to Opal and me. We've trouble on our hands. Would You please tell us what to do next?"

Opal got up from her rocker and started to stir the cabbage and meat cooking in a black iron pot over the fire.

"Miz Christy, I'm recollectin' what Granny told me 'bout Bird's Eye. His daddy didn't treat him good. Used to whup him for nothin'. When he was a real teensy boy, his daddy taught him to be such a good aim that he could drive a rifle ball through the eye of a bird. That's how he come by his name, Bird's Eye. But the young'un couldn't stomach all that hatefulness. When he was fourteen he lit out from home."

I sat down on the cricket stool by the hearth. Opal turned away from the fire to wipe her steaming face with her tattered, faded apron.

"Bird's Eye was stuck on me for awhile. One reason he's mad at Tom is because Tom courted me away.

"I seed Bird's Eye be nice once. We had gone traipsin' in the woods. Bird's Eye rifled a deer. Its fawn was hiding in the bushes. Bird's Eye threw a rock and busted one of the fawn's legs. When he started to throw another one at the fawn's head, I got fightin' mad. 'You ain't a-goin' to rock no more animals that can't fight back,' I screamed at him. When he saw I was really mad, he dropped the rock. Then he opened his knife, cut a saplin', took the baby on his lap, and splinted its poor, little, broke leg."

Opal's eyes were soft and warm, remembering. "Miz Christy, I has an idea. I'm a-goin' to mosey out to the yard and talk to the Bird's Eye that holped that little creature."

Opal untied her apron strings and walked outside. I stood in the doorway, Isaak beside me, and Vincent and Toot hanging to my skirts.

119

"You'uns must be hungry," we heard Opal say kindly. "There's some cabbage and side meat cooking in there—and hot corn pone."

Then her tone changed. "Course you're sorry fellows, and if I wasn't a woman, I'd feather into you and knock every last one of you in the next district. But then, I never did like nobody to have gnawin' stomachs, even low-down scoundrels."

The men didn't know what to say. Opal went on. "Bird's Eye, it'd be more fittin' for you, bein' head of the clan, to eat inside, comfortable-like. Miz Christy and I can bring vittles out to your kinsmen."

"Eatin' your vittles won't change nothin'," Bird's Eye grumbled.

"Looky here, Bird's Eye, I'm sure you're after Tom. Hate won't fill up your stomachs, but my hot sweet potato pie and huckleberry preserves will."

I could hear the men smacking their lips already.

"Confound it, woman. Probably I'm a consarned idiot," Bird's Eye muttered as he followed Opal to the porch.

I carried tin plates heaped with food to the men outside. When I got back inside, I found Bird's Eye eating eagerly.

"How 'bout some sass?" Opal asked him as she reached for the molasses bucket.

"Well, maybe. Right tasty," the man said between mouthfuls. "I'm near 'bout complete."

As soon as her guest's stomach was full, Opal began. "Reckon you're a-wonderin' why I asked you in. It's jest that once we'uns got along real good. And I was remembering that fawn you holped that day. Remember? I got to thinkin' bout that and I says to myself, I needs to favor Bird's Eye now."

The hard lines on Bird's Eye's face softened. I realized Opal had faith that this strange man's heart could be changed.

"Looky here, Bird's Eye, it's plumb foolish for you not to let more folks in the Cove see *that* Bird's Eye. They have the wrong idea 'bout you."

The man looked at her in genuine astonishment. "Are you a-joshin' me? Fixin' animals' legs ain't no man's work."

"Fixin' anything is man's work," Opal answered. "Tearin' down or killin', that there's easy. Any addlepated fool can pull the trigger of a rifle or fling a rock. It's *fixin'* that's hard. Course you'd have to stop killin'."

The man sat silent. "Well, Opal, you jest might have some good notions there."

Opal's words had hit the target. Bird's Eye rose to his feet, reached for his cartridges and his gun. "Tell you what I'll do," he said. "What's fittin' fer one is fittin' fer all. We'uns will lay off here for a spell. Got more business down to Allen's mill. But we'uns will be back directly."

And he walked out the door.

I spent the night with Opal and slept fitfully, knowing that David and Miss Alice didn't know where I was. Opal and I wanted to send Isaak to tell them but decided against it. We were afraid Bird's Eye or one of his men might still be watching the house.

I shared Toot's bed. We slept on a muslin mattress filled with straw and corn shucks. Every time one of us turned over, the rustling was like dry leaves crunching underfoot in the fall.

About two in the morning, we heard a soft tapping at the door. Opal opened it to find Tom and Uncle Bogg. The grandfather had found his son at Tom's favorite hunting stand deep in the woods. We huddled together by a window. There, the soft moonlight filtered through cracks in the closed shutters.

Tom looked pale and tired. "I already knowed Bird's Eye and his cronies was here, Opal," he whispered almost secretly. "No, I ain't hungry."

Tom's worried wife had just thrust a plate of warm cabbage and side meat into his lap. The same supper she had fed Bird's Eye and his kin remained warm in her pot over the smoldering fire. He pushed it aside. Tom's cheekbones stuck out and made his face look like it had two black crayon marks down each side. I wondered when he had last eaten.

"Oh, Tom, what're you going to do?" Opal plucked at her husband's sleeve.

"Opal, Tom can't fight Bird's Eye and the other Taylors by hisself. They'll kill him fer sure." Uncle Bogg scratched his bald forehead and glanced out the window nervously. "His only choice is to hide out for a while. The only two safe places he's got are jail or the mission house."

"Tom, I think you should get back to the mission. You're still not well, and we can look after you there." I reached my hand over and touched him lightly on the arm.

"Miz Christy's right, Tom. You'll be safe there with them."

Uncle Bogg leaned his leathery hands against his gun for support and stood up. "It's not safe here, son. You'd best be getting on. Back to the mission's the best place. I'll stay here with Opal and the boys."

Clumsily, Tom put one hand on his wife's shoulder. "Don't be a-fretting yerself, Opal. It'll be settled one way or the other, soon enough."

He patted her on the back and slipped out the front door while I prayed a silent prayer.

The next morning after breakfast, the children and I made it back through the woods in plenty of time for school. As we approached the mission house, I knew something was wrong. Bob Allen was walking back and forth while David shook his head. *What's Bob Allen doing here this time of the morning?* I wondered. Just then, Miss Alice came out of the mission house. She dabbed her eyes with her blue linen handkerchief.

"Christy!" David had seen me. "Where on earth were you last night? I spent half the night searching for you. Thank God, you're safe!" The look in David's eyes told me something had happened. It was a look of relief mixed with despair.

"Tom?" My lips formed the words without a sound.

"Time for school, children." David's voice was too loud. "Isaak, why don't you go on ahead?"

Isaak stood his ground. "Preacher, you ain't fooling us none. Have they got my pa?"

The compassion on David's face made me want to cry. He looked at the young boy. "All right, Isaak, you're a man. I can see that. But Toot and Vincent—"

"They ain't no babies. They've got me," the twelve-year-old said dramatically.

David pointed. "We found your father in the woods, there, just three hundred yards from the house. He almost made it back, Isaak. Someone shot him in the back." David's voice softened. "He's gone."

I sank to the ground with my skirts in the dirt and cuddled the two younger boys in my arms. Toot buried his pudgy little face in my skirt. Vincent huddled close. David put one arm around Isaak's shoulders. "You're the man of the family now."

"I want to see my pa, Preacher. Take me to him."

Without a word, David led Isaak toward the mission house.

18

Tom's murder spread a gloom over the Cove as muddy as the Big Mud Hole in the spring. Immediately, the angry feelings among the feuding families quieted down. Neither the Allen side nor the Taylor side did anything. Tom's death and funeral seemed to make a difference. A few days after the funeral, Lundy crept back to school, looking dirtier and more wild-eyed than ever. He wouldn't say a word about his father, who was still missing.

Although she was grieving, Opal seemed to be handling her husband's death well. I went to visit her often, carrying flowers or something from the kitchen. But Uncle Bogg's heart was broken. Gone were his jokes and his smiling toothless grin. The old county squire didn't know what to do. The feud no longer involved others; it had taken the life of his own son. A certain sadness now filled his tired grey eyes.

The Allen children still attended school, all except Little Burl who was getting better with each day. Bob Allen visited the mission once in a while, talking with Miss Alice or helping David finish the steeple.

By the middle of June it seemed as if things were getting back to normal. One bright summer day, Fairlight and I decided to go fishing. We grabbed our fishing lines made out of horse hair and headed for a spot we both loved. These times with Fairlight were precious to me. Our mouths watered as we talked about all the brook trout we had caught there two weeks before. We were sure we were going to fry some for supper that night.

As my friend led the way through the black-green belt of tall spruce firs, we could hear the music of the tumbling water in the distance. We made our way down a steep path winding between huckleberry bushes that skirted huge boulders. I was hoping we'd find the same weeping willow we had last found for fishing. It had been the spot out of a dream.

As we approached a large rock, my eyes suddenly caught movement. I blinked and then realized a shoulder was sticking out from one side. Fairlight saw it too, for she stopped short. "Looky, I spy . . ." But she didn't finish her sentence. The shoulder turned into a figure, which stalked directly in front of us. I drew back. The figure was Bird's Eye Taylor.

The outlaw's dirty felt hat was pulled down over his eyes. In his right hand, he held the same gun he had held at Opal's. His black beard had now grown beneath his chin, and his clothes were more tattered than ever.

"Don't aim to do you no harm." He held out a folded piece of grubby paper. "I'd be beholden if ye'd give this here to Opal." As he shoved the paper into my hands, he added, "And thank you kindly." With that, the man disappeared back around the same boulder.

Fairlight and I looked at each other in shock. We agreed that we should tell no one except Opal about this. It wouldn't help for people to know that Bird's Eye was back in the Cove. I left Fairlight and struck out for the McHone cabin.

An hour later, I handed the note to Opal. Her first reaction was surprise. "First letter ever I had," she said in wonder. "Don't know I can rightly make it all out though," she sighed. "Miz Christy, you'd best read it aloud to me."

I took the crumpled paper and read.

> Opal—it was not me that kilt Tom. When I cum back safe, I will tell it to you how it was. A friend write this for me.
>
> X BT

After I finished reading, I looked at Opal. Her eyes were filled with tears.

The following Tuesday, David and I met with Miss Alice for one of our regular talks. She stood near the stone chimney in her cabin fingering the mica glistening in the rocks. I knew she had been concerned about the effect of Tom's death on everyone. She had even canceled her regular monthly trip to Cataleechie to stay close at hand.

David was very discouraged. He felt partly responsible for Tom's murder. Perhaps he shouldn't have pressed so hard against the moonshining. Maybe Tom would still be alive.

"You know, David, we're out to win people, not war with them." The gentle lady wanted him to understand that the first step must be to change hearts. "If you clean up the pigpen and the creatures still think like pigs, the pen will soon be as dirty as ever."

"What's wrong with preaching and cleaning up the pigpen at the same time?" David gazed at the towering mountain peaks, colored orange and blue-grey in the evening sky.

Miss Alice smiled at his emotion. "I hate the moonshining as much as you. But our only choice is to get on with living and teaching and preaching the good news."

"How?" David turned around to face us.

"By showing the sinners how much we love them. Love is the better way. You see, David, love multiplies love."

I picked up one of the pillows on the sofa where I was sitting and hugged it. So many questions had plagued me since Tom's death.

"Miss Alice, why did God let this happen?" I asked. "He could've stopped it. Opal and Tom were trying to do the right thing. What happened to them doesn't look like love to me."

"No, Christy, it doesn't," Miss Alice answered as she sat down beside me. "We live in a fallen world. People make choices, and they often choose to sin. What we must remember is that God is much greater than our sin. He is love. And He cares. He cared about Tom. He cares about Opal and the children.

"His command to us is to love one another. If we had loved one another, as He loved us, Tom McHone would be alive today."

"But I'm angry. I don't know if I want to trust a God who lets bad things happen to good people."

"Christy," Miss Alice's voice was warm with feeling, "I have a word for thee. Those who've never rebelled against God, or at least shaken their fists at Him, have never known God at all."

"You mean it's good to feel these feelings?" David was as interested in her answer as I was.

She smiled at him as she sank into her red wing chair. "I mean that admitting we don't understand is the first step in finding the way God wants us to go."

"I don't seem to be able to find anything." I sighed as I scrunched the pillow against me.

"Christy, has thee ever read the Psalms?"

"No."

"King David had his troubles too. He poured out his misery in the Psalms. If you read what he wrote, you'll realize that God still loves us when we're angry and don't understand why something has happened.

"Our heavenly Father wants us to ask Him questions, and He wants us to listen for His answers. He cares about what we think and feel. His love for each of you is big enough to handle your anger. You shall see, very soon now."

Early Wednesday morning, I got up shortly before dawn and tiptoed out of the house. After our meeting with Miss Alice, I couldn't sleep. I headed for my woodland retreat on Coldsprings Mountain. The sun was just rimming the top of the far ranges, and the sky was rosy with streaks of golden light filtering through the trees. Dewdrops still glistened on the leaves. It was a beautiful June morning.

My eyes saw the beauty, but I couldn't respond to it. I was angry, and I knew it. "How can a God of love let these things happen?" I heard myself ask. "What kind of God is He?"

Bitter thoughts rolled inside me like waves in the ocean. I thought of Opal and Tom. I remembered Little Burl who'd never hurt anyone. I recalled my friend, Fairlight, and the day we had climbed to the knob. Then I'd been so sure that there was One who cares.

Crouched with my knees on the moist leaves, I cried aloud, "Why did Tom have to die? Why do these people have to hold grudges? It isn't fair." I flailed my fists in the air. "Lundy is only a boy, but he's so filled with hate. And Bird's Eye, once he could help a hurting fawn. Now, he's mean and cruel. Why? Aren't You supposed to be a God who loves His children and cares what happens to them?"

No answer came to my questions. Gradually the downpour of my words ceased. I drank in the silence. Then, ever so softly, a gentle thought touched my brain. *Your Bible, Christy. The answer is there.*

I reached behind me to find my leather-bound Bible I'd dropped in a bed of ferns. I opened to the sixth verse of Psalm 18 and read:

> In my distress I called upon the LORD . . .
> He heard my voice out of his temple,
> And my cry came before him, even into his ears.

The words reached out to me like welcoming hands across the centuries. The writer, David, had cried out to God. He had asked questions, too! I flipped over a few pages to Psalm 46.

> God is our refuge and strength,
> A very present help in trouble.

Suddenly, I stopped reading. *When David was in trouble, he had turned to God. Not only had God heard him, He had helped him!* Somehow this thought brought a revelation to my mind. *If God helped David so long ago,* my thoughts flowed like a mountain stream, *then why won't He help us? He will! That means He does care. God does care about what's happening after all!*

All my anger crumbled in the face of this reality. Feelings of love like I'd never known washed over me like a cool waterfall. Tears streamed down my cheeks. This love was real. It was personal. It was meant for me, Christy Rudd Huddleston. It was meant for the children. It was meant for Opal and Bird's Eye and Tom. Miss Alice had been right. This kind of love *was* big enough to handle any question or problem life might present. This kind of love would bring healing to a hurting world.

I had finally stepped into the reality of God's love. I had found the God who cares, truly cares for His children. Somehow I knew that everything else I needed to know would follow.

That morning, the sun came up in a blaze of glory.

19

It was early June, and school was going well. Lundy Taylor and the Allen children were all attending. Isaak McHone and his two younger brothers had returned following their father's death. David had been teaching the children Scriptures and was very pleased with their progress. Mountie's speech continued to improve. Even Creed had stopped teasing her. John Spencer and Rob Allen were doing exceptionally well, and I expected them to receive top grade honors at the end of the term. And that time was fast approaching. The end of July brought our harvest break, and I was ready.

On the Saturday of the week I had walked up to my woodland retreat, Zady Spencer streaked into the yard at the mission house.

"Zady, where have you been?" I asked as I opened the screen door. "I've missed you this week at school. In fact, I was planning to pay a visit this afternoon."

"Teacher, Ma sent me to fetch you. She needs you bad." Zady's dark eyes and thin face looked worried. I could tell something was terribly wrong.

I quickly saddled our new horse, Buttons, and we took off. When we finally rode over the crest of the last rise to the Spencer cabin, I saw the children waiting in the yard.

"Mama's inside," Clara spoke softly as she took the reins from my hands. The tall girl's face looked like stone. She wouldn't look me in the eyes.

I hurried into the cabin. Brilliant sunlight spilled across the floor, and I could see the dust particles dancing in its rays. But the cabin was so quiet it seemed deserted. Fairlight lay in her bed with a quilt tucked in around her. Her face was flushed, her eyes bloodshot and dull. Her lips and hands were so dry they had cracked.

I fought off the feelings of terror erupting like a volcano inside me.

"Where's your father?"

"Took the hound dogs and John and went bear huntin' over Laurel Top today."

Just then Fairlight raised her head off the pillow. The pupils in her eyes were dilated. She began coughing a deep, painful cough. My heart was thumping and my legs trembling. I forced myself to speak slowly to keep the panic out of my voice. "Clara, has anybody sent for Dr. MacNeill?"

"Mama didn't reckon to need no doctoring."

"You must go right now, quickly," I ordered. "Use Buttons if you need him. Zady, would you find me some rags?"

Zady brought me some cotton scraps from a quilt her mother was sewing. I dropped them into the water and pressed them on Fairlight's forehead and wrist. Somehow I had to bring down her fever. As I wrung out a rag and sponged her face, I saw brown fuzz on her teeth and tongue.

"Christy, thank you," Fairlight whispered. Then she suddenly sat up in the bed and threw off her covers. "Christy, holp me!"

I sank to my knees beside the bed and wrapped my arms around her. Her body was rigid. I began reciting the Twenty-third Psalm. The love I had found on Coldsprings Mountain poured out of me in buckets. "Though I walk through the valley of the shadow of death, I will fear no evil, for Thou art with me." I stroked her hair with my hands. Then, just as suddenly, she relaxed in my arms and stopped breathing.

Clara rushed into the cabin followed by Dr. MacNeill. My cry told them what had happened. The children began to bawl. I cradled the little ones in my arms. Clara threw herself on her mother, sobbing. Little Zady began hugging her mother's feet.

The doctor gently covered Fairlight's face with the blanket. "It's typhoid, Christy. She's had it a good ten days. There's nothing we can do for her now."

I waited until evening when Jeb returned. Then the doctor rode me back to the mission house. I barely remembered the ride. My dear, dear Fairlight was gone.

Two weeks later, Dr. MacNeill sat wearily in the parlor with David. "What looks like beautiful, sparkling drinking water may contain billions of typhoid bacilli," I heard him say as I walked in. "If a spring or creek is at the bottom of the hill, every nasty thing is washed into it." I remembered the last time David and Dr. MacNeill had been in this parlor after Tom was shot, and I was glad the two of them were talking again.

Before Fairlight, I had never seen a person sick with typhoid fever, but I'd heard a lot about it. The mountain people called it "the summer scourge." It was very contagious, spread by deadly bacteria passing from one person to another. Often the fever began as soon as warm weather brought spring waters to spread the filth down the mountains and flies to carry the germs.

After Fairlight's funeral I felt numb, but I couldn't stay that way for long. Within a week, more than fifty-four people had come down with the dreaded disease. Miss Alice and I read medical books and gathered items for a medical kit. We quickly realized that one doctor couldn't treat every patient, so we started traveling from cabin to cabin. We cleaned dishes and spoon-fed the sick in beds crawling with flies. I washed dirty clothing in lye soap and boiled linens that hadn't been cleaned for weeks. Miss Alice and I carried endless heavy pails of water, bathing folks three and four times a day. I held my nose when I buried the urine and stools in deep trenches in the woods so the typhoid germs wouldn't spread.

Although Dr. MacNeill was hopeful this wouldn't turn into an epidemic, we set up a cot for him in David's quarters.

"Should I cancel school?" I asked him one night as we sat in the parlor.

"Your children will be as safe at school as they would be at home," he replied through a ring of pipe smoke swirling around his head. "Safer in fact because the school's cleaner."

"I agree, Christy. Thee should continue." Miss Alice had just walked in with a tray of cool ice tea. "And I've been thinking, we should let some of the children board here for now. I know Isaak wants to help us. And with Bird's Eye still at large, we really need to keep Lundy."

I winced at the thought. Lundy? But I knew Miss Alice was right. After all, he was still a boy and he needed someone who cared.

Two days later, I was reading a story to Creed and Zacharias when Isaak rushed up to my desk. "Teacher, Teacher, he's a-bleeding!"

I jerked my head up to see Lundy slumped over a desk. Blood was pouring from his nose. I dashed down the aisle. "On the floor, Lundy. Lie down!" I ordered. "Yes, that's it." I noticed that his pimply skin was blotched with pink and white. It took a long time for the bleeding to stop. Once it had, however, the big boy grinned up at me with his yellow teeth. I could see that he was starved for attention.

"Isaak, would you take Lundy to the mission house and ask Miss Ida to put him to bed? Tell her that Dr. Mac-Neill should see him when he returns this afternoon."

That afternoon, the doctor stopped by. "Not much question, Christy. It's typhoid all right. Now we do have a situation on our hands."

I pushed aside the papers I was grading. My old desk wobbled beneath my arms. "Isn't it dangerous for Isaak and Ruby Mae and the other children now boarding with us?"

"Dangerous for everybody."

"Should we send them home?"

"Probably. But first we need medicine, and I don't have enough in my saddlebags. There's plenty over at my place, but I have two other calls to make this afternoon. Would you ride over and get it?"

I glanced out one of the side windows. Clouds had been building all day. They were now towering thunderheads, dark and threatening. I knew what I had to do. "Of course I'll go," I answered.

"Then I'll write you out a list so you'll know what to bring." He pulled out a piece of paper and began to scribble.

20

The thunder
rolled and rum-
bled and crack-
led as I raced
on horseback
to the doctor's.
I threw my body
against the cabin door,
and the wind and rain almost blew me inside. The door
flew open. With my back, I slammed the door closed and
leaned hard against it to catch my breath.

Smells of stale tobacco, leather, and burned bacon
grease caught my nose. The doctor hadn't been at home
for some time. The locked room was somewhere to my
right. I remembered that spring afternoon I had spent
here while David was at Lufty Branch Church. I wondered then what secrets lay behind the locked door. Now
I was going to find out.

As I moved, my right leg banged into something, and
I almost fell over. As lightning flashed I saw that it was
a chest. I rubbed my leg. A loud growl of thunder star-

tled me. Lightning zigzagged across the sky. I walked with one hand stretched out to keep from hitting anything else. Then I slid my fingers over the wall to locate the door and then the keyhole. There it was.

My heart beat fast as my fingers pulled the old-fashioned brass key from my jacket and fit it into the lock. I turned it to the right, and the door swung open. An odor of chemicals bombarded me. I had to find a lamp. Cautiously I stretched out one hand and moved it in an arc to find an oil lamp sitting on a shelf to my right. With matches from a nearby canister, I removed the glass chimney and lighted the wick.

Lifting the lamp, I scanned the room eagerly. I drew in my breath. I was in a laboratory! In the middle of the floor stood a stool and table with a microscope, an alcohol lamp, beakers, and a lot of other equipment. Against the wall to my right were cabinets with shallow drawers. Another wall was covered with charts. At the far end of the room, shelves had been built floor to ceiling. One section had books, while the others held bottles of medicine and pills.

A floorboard creaked under my feet, and I jumped. I looked over my shoulder almost expecting to see someone behind me. The yellow light from the lamp flickered over the walls and ceiling. I pulled open one drawer to find many slides, all carefully arranged and numbered. I realized years of work were contained in these files. *Dr. MacNeill is using this room for research!*

This was not the room of an ordinary backwoods doctor. Admiration and respect rose in me. The doctor *did* care about these people. Behind closed doors, he was working to find cures for their physical problems. He knew the mountain folks wouldn't understand, so he didn't tell them.

I carried the lamp to the shelves of bottles. Each jar and bottle had been carefully labeled. I took the list of wanted drugs out of my pocket. The doctor's instructions had been very clear, "In no case bring it all, Christy. I can't have my private supply stripped of any one drug."

Quickly I poured some of the medicine into sterile containers, returned the lamp to its shelf, blew out the flame, closed and locked the door.

Outside, it was still raining, but only softly now. After carefully arranging the medicines in the saddlebags, I pulled the front door shut after me, mounted, and galloped toward the mission.

The next morning, Dr. MacNeill arrived early at the mission house. His clothes were wrinkled, his face deeply lined with worry. He looked as if he had not slept for days.

"Situation doesn't look good," he said to Miss Alice and me as we walked into the parlor with him. Miss Ida and David followed closely behind. "Two new cases again yesterday. They're so scattered we'll never find the source." Absently he ran his fingers through the back of his unwashed hair. "I need to make sure you all understand exactly what to do. I know you've been helping, but this is vital."

Miss Ida groaned, thinking about all the extra work.

"You'll have to clean Lundy's room with disinfectant. And after you've handled anything—*anything* in there, you must wash your hands with a solution I'll make up for you. All Lundy's linens have to be soaked for two hours in carbolic acid, then boiled and washed in lye soap."

We listened to the doctor's orders like soldiers before a battle. "David, your job will be to bury the urine and stools in a deep trench in the woods. They're pure cultures of typhoid bacilli and will spread the fever quicker than anything. And Christy, it's time now to close school for a while. Send the other children home."

That night, the sick boy complained of a raging headache over his eyes. His fever rose to 103° and stayed there. Miss Alice spoon-fed him every half hour. She raced up and down the stairs bringing beef bouillon or milk with sugar. Often he pushed the food away, and she had to force it between his lips.

I watched the gentle Quaker lady change the bed linens and rinse the boy's mouth and tongue so typhoid sores wouldn't form. I helped her carry pails of water and sponge bathe him four times a day to try to bring down the fever. It seemed endless. By Saturday morning, she was red-eyed and barely awake.

"A fine thing," Miss Ida said as she placed a plate of pancakes in front of Miss Alice. She didn't like having Lundy as a patient. "Don't care a mouse's hair about that boy, but I do care about you, Alice Henderson. Get over to your place and sleep. I'll nurse him now."

"And I'll take the night shift," I told her.

When I entered his room at ten o'clock that night, I found Lundy in an old patched nightshirt Miss Ida had found somewhere. His eyes were open, but he didn't recognize me. What followed was the slowest night of my life. No sooner would I sink into the easy chair to try to sleep than the boy would moan or cry out for water. More than once, I had just fallen asleep when a terrible stench would wake me up. I would drag myself out of the chair to change the boy's bed linens and nightclothes. Then I would scrub myself with scalding hot water and the carbolic acid solution. Miss Ida's battered alarm clock told me the time. It was only ten minutes past twelve.

Time inched by like a slow earthworm crawling up the stump of a rotting tree. I worked like a wind-up toy and lost track of how many times I was up and down through the night. Finally, sometime near dawn it began to drizzle. The rhythm of the rain lulled both Lundy and me to sleep.

Then I was awakened by the sound of knocking. I sat up and realized it came from the back door. I waited, hoping Miss Ida would hear it, but she didn't. At last, I forced my legs to walk down the stairs. At the back door, I turned the key, slid the bolt, and opened the door partway. I drew back, startled. Bird's Eye Taylor stared back at me in the rain.

Bird's Eye had returned because he had heard about Lundy. "Ain't got no stomach left for hidin' out," he told us later at breakfast. "Is he took bad?"

David sipped a cup of steaming coffee. I could tell from the look on his face that he was suspicious. He knew this mountain man's heart was as tough as a leather hide. This could all be an act. Miss Ida's loud banging of the heavy iron skillet told me she wasn't too happy either.

"He's been very sick, Bird's Eye," Miss Alice chimed in, trying to ease the tension a bit.

"I'd like to stay and help for a spell."

I bit my lower lip and waited for Miss Alice's response. "We appreciate your offer," she replied, "but you're still wanted for Tom's murder. We won't hide you from the law."

"I knowed that when I snuck back." The man fingered his grubby black hat. He looked at the floor and then into her eyes. "I'm tired of running."

The next morning, I was sitting on the front steps resting my feet and enjoying the mountain air. I could hear David and Dr. MacNeill through the open window in the parlor. "Who does he think he is?" David asked. "Why should we be taken in by a murderer? Or his no-good son?"

There was a long silence. Then the doctor's voice. "I understand how you feel, David. But when I took the Hippocratic oath, I swore to do my best to save lives, and that's what I must do for Lundy. The rest will just have to work itself out. And right now, we need Bird's Eye's help."

21

By the second week, Lundy's temperature was dropping toward normal. He began to eat again. In fact, he wanted to eat all the time. "I been lying here smacking my mouth thinkin' of hot corn pone and a thick piece of ham meat," he told me one morning when I changed his bed linens. "Can't I have some licorice sticks?"

"You'll get all that soon enough." I was feeling very tired this morning and I had a headache, so I didn't want to deal with him today.

My hand bumped into something under the mattress. I pulled out a sack of hard candy.

"Where'd you get this, Lundy?"

"Ain't telling."

"You know you're not supposed to have it."

"Aw, no harm can come from a little candy."

Later that day, I told Dr. MacNeill that Lundy was getting harder to handle. He gathered all of us in the parlor. Miss Ida pursed her lips and stood at the window with her arms crossed in front of her. Having Bird's Eye around still didn't please her. David looked like a puppy dog without his master. He could pray for people and encourage them, but he didn't know how to care for the sick. And he still didn't trust Bird's Eye, who was sitting on the soft sofa chewing a piece of straw.

The doctor spoke directly to him. "Bird's Eye, Lundy must not eat any solid food. The walls of his intestines are very thin now. If he eats solid food too soon, the food can tear holes inside him and he can bleed to death. Got that?"

"Doc, I'll try, but the youngster has a mighty way 'bout gettin' what he wants."

"Bird's Eye, you have to help us keep your son in line. He's going to want to eat everything in sight. If we let him, he may die. Think you can handle him?"

"Shore. If he gets to rippin' around, I'll smack the fire out of him."

The next morning, I walked to my woodland retreat. While sitting on the ledge, I drank in the blues and pinks of the early morning sky. The walk had been very hard and my legs ached. My head throbbed. *I'm tired*, I told myself. *I'd best get back.*

No sooner had I reached the front door of the mission house, than I could hear footsteps running down the stairs. I opened the door to see Miss Ida carrying a pail of water.

"What's wrong?" I yelled to her.

"It's Lundy. Awful sick."

I didn't even wait to take off my shawl before climbing the stairs. I found Miss Alice grilling the boy with questions. "Lundy, have you eaten anything that you shouldn't?"

"Naw."

Just then, Miss Ida returned. "I found what you want to know," she told Miss Alice. "I'd hard-boiled a dozen eggs and left them in a pan on the table. Two are gone."

"Ow!" Lundy groaned. "It hurts. Oh, my left side . . ."

For the first time, I saw Miss Alice look frightened. "If only Neil were here. He's all the way across the river near Lyleton. He won't be back for another three hours. The only thing we can do is to turn him on his right side."

By noon, Lundy's temperature had dropped seven degrees. He was turning blue. I knew this meant he was going into shock. Bird's Eye got his hog rifle and fired a blast out of the window to try to wake his son up. It did no good. Miss Alice kept feeling his pulse and wiping his forehead. "If only Neil would come!" she moaned.

Around two o'clock, we heard someone at the front door. I ran to the top of the stairs. It was Dr. MacNeill and David. One look at my face and the doctor came bounding up the stairs. I stayed in the hall with David to tell him what had happened. When we walked in the room, the doctor sat by the bed with his hand on the boy's pulse. His face was set in grim lines.

Miss Alice stood at his elbow. Without turning his head, I heard him whisper, "Saying a prayer, Alice?"

"Yes, Neil, I was."

The doctor put Lundy's hand down, felt his chest and listened to it. "It's all over." He turned to Lundy's father who had been standing at the foot of the bed. Bird's Eye was gone.

22

Around the supper table that evening, no one talked. As I toyed with the food on my plate, I wondered whether Bird's Eye would blame us for his son's death. Where had he gone? Would he run away again?

My questions were answered soon after supper. Bird's Eye showed up. All of us except Dr. MacNeill were sitting in the parlor when he suddenly appeared in the doorway.

"Been a-trompin' and a-trompin'," he began, speaking directly to Miss Alice.

She drew him into the room. "We're glad you decided to come back, Bird's Eye. The doctor did everything he could. We're so very sorry."

"Oh, I ain't faulting none of you, ma'am. Doc either. Couldn't nobody do nothin' for that boy. Never could learn him nothin' . . ." He ran his hand over the stubble on his face. When he wouldn't sit down, I realized he had something important to say.

"No need to let no grass grow under my feet," Bird's Eye pulled off his hat and fingered the holes in it. "I want you'uns to know the truth. It warn't me who kilt Tom." His voice trailed off.

"That day Opal fed me, she said most any fool could pull a trigger but that it took a man to fix things. Well, got to thinkin' on that considerable. Me and my boys left Opal's place and shoved for Bob Allen's mill, but he warn't there. Studied on it some more. Knowed she was right. I couldn't do no good a-killin'. So I took my kin back up the mountain to my place.

"Lundy'd gone traipsin'. He come in later packin' my old hog rifle and squawkin' that he'd kilt Tom. Said how he'd helped me a'fore by stopping those children from pesterin' under the schoolhouse. He'd done good by tellin' me 'bout Bob Allen rattin' on us to the preacher. And now he'd gotten rid of the traitor for good."

"Just a minute," David's voice boomed across the room. "You're blaming Tom's murder on a boy who's dead!"

The mountaineer's eyes turned to steel and he lowered his brows. "You ain't believin' me?" he said in a much deeper tone.

David's lips curled in scorn. "What proof do you have?"

"Don't reckon I got none." He hesitated and looked toward Miss Alice.

Miss Alice leaned forward in her chair. The light of a nearby lamp flickered across the soft wrinkle lines in her face. "I have proof, David. I've known for a month that Lundy shot Tom."

Every eye turned toward her.

"Just after Lundy got sick, Bob Allen came to see me. He said he was concerned about our nursing Lundy here. Said he knew something that was weighing on him." She paused, smoothed the creases in her navy cotton skirt, and then rested her gaze on Bird's Eye.

"Bird's Eye, the night you left the McHones and went to Bob's mill, Bob was on his way to David's bunkhouse. At the edge of the mission woods, he heard the shot that killed Tom and he saw Lundy running away. Nobody else was around."

The mountain man stared back at her in silent amazement. "Saw him for shore?"

"Yes. For sure."

"But he wouldn't help me. He be an Allen." The man's face dropped.

"Bird's Eye, if Bob didn't mean to help, he wouldn't have told me. Bob and I have had many talks. He hasn't found hatred very good food either."

This was almost too much for Bird's Eye. It was like a sledge hammer smashing a mighty boulder to bits. *This is one of those great moments,* I thought to myself. *When Opal fed Tom's enemies that day, she showed them love. She stepped out in faith by speaking the words rising within her. And like an arrow they met their mark. And Miss Alice, all the time she was nursing Lundy, she knew. She knew! But she loved him anyway.*

Later, Bird's Eye headed toward the McHones to tell Opal. My mind was foggy, and I had trouble listening to David and Miss Alice, who were talking in the kitchen. "I've got a lot of thinking to do," he told her. "I stepped in where I didn't belong. I wanted to believe the worst. I haven't been any help at all."

"Nothing stings like hurt pride, David," she said calmly. "You must go to the Lord. He will heal thee."

Suddenly, the room whirled around me. I reached out toward the table to steady myself. Dizzy! So dizzy! As I fell forward, a glass shattered on the floor.

I heard David's voice far in the distance, "Christy!"

The blankets were crushing me. I wanted to get them off. My tongue felt dry and swollen, too large for my mouth. *Water would taste good. Where is the water? I want some water. But first I must open my eyes.*

I was in my room, but it looked different. Some of the pieces of furniture had been moved out. There were not even any curtains at the windows. A lot of bottles lined the table.

Miss Alice was bending over me. I looked up into her face, "Am I sick?"

"I've been waiting for you to wake up to give you a drink. You're going to be fine, Christy."

My eyelids were so heavy they shut themselves. I opened my mouth when I felt the spoon touch my lips. The cool liquid trickled across my tongue and down my throat.

Day melted into night. Night into day. People came and went. They kept opening my mouth and pouring liquid down my throat. Someone was always fussing with my covers and washing my body.

Dr. MacNeill's face was nearby. I wanted to talk to him, but it was too hard. He had gentle hands. Now he was pressing my side. That hurt. *Why is he poking my stomach?*

Hours . . . days. Light . . . darkness. Sunlight . . . moonlight. Time. What was time? Everything seemed the same.

I can hear voices. Isn't that David? Wait a minute. There's Bird's Eye. He has a gun. David! Watch out! Watch out! Oh, and there's Fairlight. She's walking along the bank of that stream flowing through the meadow. Fairlight! Can you hear me? She's barefoot, wearing her blue gingham dress. She looks so happy. But she can't see me. Why can't she see me? Now, someone is calling my name. Who is that?

"Christy, Christy!" I knew that voice. "Can you hear me?"

My eyelids were latched together with iron bolts. They were so heavy. I struggled to pry them open. A sliver of light shone through. I blinked. Everything was so hazy. *Where am I? And whose voice is that?*

"Christy, can you see me?"

It was Dr. MacNeill. He sat beside my bed holding my left hand. I blinked again. Slowly, the room came into focus. Miss Alice and David and even Miss Ida stood silently at the foot of my bed. I tried to swallow. My tongue cooperated.

"Christy," the doctor said gently. "Can you hear me?"

I nodded.

"Well, mercy sakes, child," Miss Ida exclaimed, "you sure had me worried for awhile. Didn't know as I was going to see your smiling face ever again."

"We've been praying for thee, Christy," Miss Alice added, "but I knew your work here wasn't over yet." Her smile washed over me like a refreshing rain. It felt good to see her.

David stepped forward. "The children have been bringing all these flowers and berries," he said. "I've been in here too, praying for God to bring you back. You've been very sick."

"But you're going to be fine now." Dr. MacNeill stood up and stretched. "The worst is over." He took a deep breath and squared his shoulders.

"How long have I had typhoid?" I managed to whisper.

Miss Alice sat down on my bed. "Nearly two weeks now. The children have been asking about thee every day. David and I managed to start school again and carry on, but it's been a task. We missed you!"

Dr. MacNeill walked to the door. "You rest now, Christy."

"You need your strength." Miss Ida chimed in. "The last day of school is just around the corner, and we've much to do!"

23

The fresh July air poured in through my open windows. I had been back at school for a week. Then I remembered. *Today is the last day of school!* As I lay in bed, my mind traveled back to that snowy January morning seven months ago when the schoolchildren and I had first met. So much had happened in these seven short months.

After breakfast, I walked over to the schoolroom early. It had never been so clean. My pupils had washed the windows and decorated the room with rhododendron leaves, cinnamon ferns, wild lilies, and branches of red elderberry bushes picked high in the mountains. Between the leaves and ferns, I had tacked up the nicest drawings and maps, the papers with the highest grades, and some outstanding arithmetic papers.

Soon the room was crowded to the doors with parents standing along the walls. Opal McHone sat with her boys in one row. The Holts and the Allens were there. I spotted the Spencers and greatly missed Fairlight. It wouldn't be the same without her. Ben Pentland had settled in the back with his mailbag dropped at his feet. Miss Ida, dressed in her best black dress buttoned high at the neck, sat in a chair David had carried over from the mission house. Miss Alice and Dr. MacNeill stood beside one of the open windows.

David opened the program. "Mothers and fathers, boys and girls, this is a big day for our school. After the exercises are over, during refreshments, we hope you'll wander around and look at the samples of work posted on the walls. And now, first on our program is a welcome from Mountie O'Teale."

Mountie was dressed in a clean, starched, gingham dress, her hair neatly combed, and her eyes sparkling with excitement. She spoke slowly but clearly. "Fathers and mothers, . . . we are glad you . . . have come today. We hope . . . you like . . . our program. We hope . . . that you have . . . a good time."

It was a proud moment for Mountie and for me. She had not stuttered at all. This Mountie was a different child from the defeated Mountie of seven months ago. The little girl looked at me with triumph in her eyes. I smiled back, forming the word "good!" with my lips and nodding my head in approval.

The program continued with some rousing mountain singing. A number of the children recited poetry they had memorized.

"And next we have Creed Allen," I enthusiastically announced.

The onlookers craned their necks to watch Creed proudly march to the front with his raccoon riding on one shoulder. He had never lost sight of the pact I had made with him that first day of school.

"Now ain't that a sight in the world!" one father exclaimed. "Never saw nothin' like that!" another voiced. Most of the men in the room thought raccoons were good for nothing but killing.

From his pocket Creed pulled out a thin rock shining with bits of mica. "See this, Scalawag?"

The masked creature stretched out an eager paw for it. "No, not yet. Turn around, Scalawag. Zacharias, come up here, will ya, and keep him a-lookin' the other way."

Zacharias bounded up, delighted to be a part of the show. Creed buried the fragment carefully under a tall stack of papers on my desk. "Now Scalawag, ye can start searchin'. Rassel up the rock."

The little animal seemed to understand that this was a game. He scurried over to the desk to lift papers. The children cheered. Finally, Scalawag found the piece of glittering rock and stood on the desk examining it with his paws.

"Now I'll tell ye about coons," Creed began.

"Rrrrr—" Creed's voice was drowned by loud growling and furious barking. Two hound dogs streaked toward the front of the room, rushing the coon. The children shrieked. Scalawag leaped from the top of the desk to Creed's head, hanging on to his hair and screeching frantically as the dogs reached Creed and began leaping and clawing at his legs. The children were out of their seats now, flinging themselves in turn on the dogs.

"Scat, you hound!" they screamed. Creed yelled the loudest, "Quit that tryin' to shinny up me. I ain't no tree."

Jeb Spencer bounded forward. "Jasper, settle there! Big Ed, I'll lay my hand to you. Down, dog!" He hit Big Ed, and the dog whined and backed away. The dogs were confused. Rushing coons usually pleased their master. They had smelled coon, so they'd gone after coon. But now Jeb was herding them away. "Numskull hound dogs. They bark big, but they bite small," he murmured to the onlookers.

The uproar didn't dampen anyone's spirits, however. After everyone had settled down, Creed finished his talk about coons, and then David announced, "Now the children will recite Scripture verses they have selected."

Zady Spencer recited the Twenty-fourth Psalm. Rob Allen said part of the eighth chapter of Romans. Little Burl spoke the familiar "For God so loved the world . . ." And then Sam Houston Holcombe stood up. With a confident grin, he began reeling off from Genesis 11. "These are the generations of Shem: Shem was an hundred years old, and begat Arphaxad two years after the flood: . . ."

David started to protest, then quickly reached for a Bible off my desk and began flipping pages.

"And Arphaxad lived five and thirty years, and begat Salah: . . ."

"And Salah lived thirty years, and begat Eber: . . ."

David checked every line the nine-year-old was saying. He couldn't believe it. How could any child correctly recite those passages with all those difficult names? The little boy's voice went on and on, emphasizing only one word, the all-important *begat*.

The blond-haired child marched through all the verses to the end of chapter 11. David looked amazed. He had offered a prize for the most verses. The audience reacted with wild enthusiasm. When Miss Alice presented a new Bible to the proud Sam Houston, the crowd cheered.

Finally, refreshment time arrived. Miss Alice walked up to the front.

"Friends, last January a young woman who had never taught school came to us. In her heart was the dream of helping boys and girls. We have now seen the beginning of that dream. We've had the longest school term ever seen in Cutter Gap, and it's been a great term. Christy Huddleston, would thee please come up?"

As I rose from my seat, the room erupted in applause. I looked around at the mass of faces, still dirty and grimy. Yet today, I couldn't see the dirt. I could only see the love. Suddenly, as I walked toward Miss Alice, it all made sense. I had found my answer.

Thank You, Lord, for bringing me here, my heart prayed as I opened the gift Miss Alice handed me. It was a deer, whittled and carved out of a single piece of wood, smoothed and polished.

"John Spencer did it," she whispered softly. "He wanted it to be from everyone. He worked on it for three months."

Words lodged like chestnuts in my throat. I belonged. Among these mountain people, my life was counting for something, and it felt good. Miss Alice's words returned to my soul. This kind of heart love did bring miracles, and the biggest miracle of all was in me.